William Money Hardinge

The Willow-Garth

Vol. II

William Money Hardinge

The Willow-Garth
Vol. II

ISBN/EAN: 9783337065201

Printed in Europe, USA, Canada, Australia, Japan

Cover: Foto ©Andreas Hilbeck / pixelio.de

More available books at **www.hansebooks.com**

THE
WILLOW - GARTH

A Novel

BY

WILLIAM M. HARDINGE

AUTHOR OF 'EUGENIA' AND 'CLIFFORD GRAY'

IN TWO VOLUMES

VOL. II.

LONDON

RICHARD BENTLEY & SON, NEW BURLINGTON ST.

Publishers in Ordinary to Her Majesty the Queen

1886

Printed by R. & R. CLARK, *Edinburgh.*

G., C., & Co

CONTENTS OF VOLUME II.

BOOK THE THIRD

CUSTOM

BOOK THE FOURTH

CONTEMPT

BOOK THE THIRD

CUSTOM

19

' Love bindeth '

CHAPTER I.

WALDINE WRITES

John—

—*Mon ami* John!—I have something of the greatest importance to tell you. I must say it at once: it will not be kept back. And it matters *so much*. Presently I will tell you all about everything else and all about the least of things, *me*; but first I must write you the all-important news. It is this, John: 'I love you,—I love you,—I love you!'

And now I've written it, there seems nothing more to say; for what else can matter, what else is worth telling, in comparison of this?

'I think of you!' that seems to come next

best : I think of you in your home.   Already
I have seen something in London that has
reminded me of you.   I have looked out of
the window : it rains, and the pavement is
black with wet, and on the dark gloss there is
a bright shine of lamplight.   John, when Mrs.
Lupton and I drove past your little house
there was just that light upon its windows.
The sunset glare, reflected on the blackness of
the window-glass, shone like a flame on coal.
When I look at the murky pavement here, and
the lamplight flares upon it, I shall think of
your home always.

Ah ! my love, when shall I not think of it,
when not think of you ?   Is there any other
subject of thought but this in all the world ?

You want to know about me : it seems
absurd, but I believe you do.   John, what is
there that you want to know ?   Invent it, I
will subscribe to it gladly ; but on my life I
can find nothing worth the telling.   Have
you not invented me ? — I am so wholly
different to my old self that indeed I think
so !—well, then ! you can invent a story of my

days, and I—I will only say to you,—' I love
you !—it is true ! '

Your face follows me for ever : if I were dead
it would lead me from my grave. Have you not
lifted me up from darkness to light, Orpheus—
Orpheus—with your song of love ? While you
sing to me shall I ever cease to follow, ' as the
water follows the moon, silently, with fluid steps,
anywhere around the globe.' Sing on ' Oh
singer, bashful and tender ! . . . I hear your call.'

Some of which is out of a book Mrs.
Lupton gave me to read in the train. Was
it not written of you ?

And now, for you are looking very impatient,
you face that draws my heart, I will try to
write you categorically what has befallen us.

Coming home from the tableaux, I attempted
to tell Aunt Linda something about you : John,
you cannot conceive how difficult it was to
do so. At first I think she fancied that I
was your messenger to *her*, for she only
said, ' What a pity it is that I have been induced to act !' But when I insisted on it that
you—how shall I say it ?—liked *me*, she was

very angry, and thought it 'quite ridiculous.'
Then I said that I—'liked'—you, and she said
she did not wonder;—that you were . . . no!
I will not tell you, for fear I should make you
vain! Next she remembered that I had told
her you cared for *me*, and she left off praising
you and only said the affair was very odd
and very unfortunate, and that she must beg
of me not to distress her darling saint about
it. On this point she was so impressive that
I promised not to speak to his lordship till she
gave me leave : else certainly I should have
gone and waked him from his sleep to tell him.

What prevailed most with Aunt Linda
was her fatigue : by the time we reached
home she had, I really think, forgotten all I
had told her, and her 'good-night' to me in
the hall was the farewell of a martyr at the
stake. 'It's over!' she said tragically, 'it's
done; it will be in every paper to-morrow.
And now for rest.' For half an instant I
imagined she was speaking of *us*—(don't you
think those two wavy letters are the prettiest
in the whole alphabet ?)—I too thought 'It is

over ! it is done !' but I did not sleep—unless, indeed, it is all a sleep and you the king of dreams ! . . .

In the morning Stéphanie came to me with two announcements. The first, that I was to go to her ladyship before I went downstairs ; the second, that his lordship was much less well and you had driven over to Newton for the doctor. I thought, at the moment, that it was only a *ruse* to prevent our meeting ; but I do not think so now. I think that there is something almost divine in Aunt Linda's foolishness—that it is just because she does nothing and plans nothing that she always gets her own way. She is like a feather on the wind, but the wind blows fair at the feather's will.

I went to her room at once : she was in bed, with a hand-glass and a pile of notes by her side. I think she looks at herself constantly, while she writes them, in order to be quite certain that she describes herself accurately in each one of them. She was very serious about Lord Grenvers—that sudden change to frost

had brought on agonies of neuralgia and he
could not bear to be spoken to.—John, if you
are ever ill I will talk to you till you are well or
dead, but I will not nurse you, and I will not let
any one else nurse you.   This is *par parenthèse.*—About *us* (observe again the beauty of
the word !) she said no syllable.   On the con-
trary, she told me to go out for a walk.   I
walked to our ash-tree, and somehow expected
to find it still golden.   Its bareness made me
sad.   You, the sight of whom would have caused
it to blossom like Aaron's rod, were away at
Newton.   And for two hours I roamed the
woods in vain.   It was icily cold and the day
was empty and dark.   I came back to luncheon
—so long ago, it seems, is it possible that it
was only yesterday ?—I was told that I must
lunch with her ladyship upstairs.   To my
amazement, she was dressed and in the best of
spirits : I felt a wretch beside her, chilled and
lonely as I was.   She jumped for joy when I
came into the room.

'Oh ! here you are !' she said.   'Is not
Charlotte an angel ? Her tableaux have bored

her to such an extent that she's off to London to-night for a fortnight's fun ; she sent to ask me to come with her, but of course I can't leave Grenvers, so—never say I'm not a good aunt !—I told her you would go instead, and Stéphanie is packing your things already.'

I said I did not want to go. She answered that I must : she said his lordship cannot bear the thought of any one being in the house during these attacks, which often make him cry aloud with pain.—' I am such a believer in Providence,' she profanely added, ' that I recognise Charlotte's trip as providential. And just think what would become of us all if we flew in the face of Providence !'

She made such a clever little gesture of flying, and looked so pretty, that I believe I burst out laughing. A moment later I felt inclined to cry, but she gave me no time. We lunched in her boudoir—where *you* were once—and all of a sudden, as if you were a topic of every-day conversation, she touched on you. She said, ' As soon as ever my dear saint is better, I shall speak to him about your future and its advancement.' I wanted, now I think of it, to say a thousand things, but I could not. It seemed irreverent: I did not even thank her. I cannot tell indeed if she be thankworthy or not.

And all the rest of the afternoon I was in such a whirl that I scarcely recollect what happened. Mrs. Lupton arrived at half-past three, and was with Aunt Linda while I got ready. We left Netherfield by the 4.40 train, and were established and at dinner here by a quarter-past nine. John, you have never been to London, have you? I thought not; it is such a dreary place. It is entirely empty—empty as the grave—because you are not here. It is quite cold and quite dark, whereas at Whiteknyghts it is sunshine and summer—sunshine and summer for ever;—until you come up to see me here, and then Whiteknyghts will be cold and dark and the sunshine and summer will be here, . . . because of *you*.

This house is charming: I never imagined that a town-house could be so pretty; it is warm as a nest; even the staircase is as full of ornaments as Aunt Linda's boudoir. And there are Netherfield flowers in every room. I feel as if I were an enchanted princess. But I want to be free from my bondage : I am tired out already of the fairy palace.

. . . Ah! my love, my love! how is it with you in the house with the sunlit windows —the house which I have never entered and which you have never left? Have you any memory there of me, who love you so, to bear you company? You have your books, your songs, your pursuits. Do they leave you any moment for the remembrance of me? In your full days is there dwelling-room for my poor intrusive ghost? Answer me ; for indeed I have no other home than in your heart. Do you know, in any way, the possession of me that you have taken? Do you know that I want to make all claims upon you, to tell you everything, to have you wholly mine? That is a little bit of what I wish, and the rest of it . . . ah! the sweet rest!—

'And the rest' I cannot tell you to-day, because Mrs. Lupton is calling me. She is great at organising things, and she has a bachelor friend in town whom she has driven in a hansom to see. He appears to have been at home, and they have made a plan for to-night into which I perforce enter—I who should like to sit here all the evening and think of you.

For I am happy, have no fear! something you said to me that night was wrong: 'You will want riches, pleasures, friends.' John, I am not like that. I want nothing but you. —After all, *were* you wrong? will you not be all in all to me, your joys my riches, your tastes my pleasures, your thoughts my friends? . . . Ah! yes, at least let your thoughts befriend me.—*Sans adieu,*

WALDINE DE STAIR.

—And the beginning and the end is this: 'I love you.'

CHAPTER II.

IN CURZON STREET

WALDINE'S letter, although as a recital inadequate, tells sufficiently well what befell her as a sequel to the little wind's suggestion, Mrs. Lupton proving the *deus ex machinâ* of that Providence which Lady Grenvers flattered with her trust.

Her ladyship, for all her *naïveté*, had sufficient wit to see that she had thrown her niece overmuch into the company of a man who could not remain unmoved by her beauty: unable at the moment to betake herself to her husband's counsel, she had appealed to her neighbour's, but, with an instinct against Mrs. Lupton's sarcasm, she had not told that lady even as much as she suspected of Waldine's *tocquade,* whereas Mrs. Lupton imagined that more was made of the affair than need be. She was interested and amused, though she was not in the least serious. But she had taken a fancy to Val, and she was good-natured enough to hurry her departure to get the girl out of Lord Grenvers' way during the period of his pain. It was his pain which had most weight with her. Moreover, she liked sudden flights and impromptu plans. The flights had a mysterious air, which gave her a reputation for Bohemianism in the county. She made them alone, sometimes, just for the sake of the talk and stir that they caused. Curzon Street was always ready and there was generally something at the theatres; it was good for the few servants she left in London to be taken by surprise—the larger staff at Netherfield would be occupied in setting the rooms to rights after their disarrangement;—Mr. Collington and the other 'second selves' could do the honours to her departing guests, whom also it was no small joy to mystify; and she could see one or two newspaper men in London to describe her 'classic and oriental pictures' to them by word of mouth, which might or might not add colour to their reports.

In the meantime she said nothing to Waldine about John Lyne. Mrs. Lupton was a woman of her word, and she had promised Lady Grenvers not to enter on the topic. In her heart of hearts she was rather *intriguée* and would incline to foster this fancy and not to crush it ; she was not unaware of the fostering effect of silence while she kept silence. Silence was in her bond, but that the silence should signify approval or disapproval had not been stated.

'Who is it,' she had said to Waldine in the train, 'who says that love "keeps out the cold better than a cloak, it serves for food and raiment?" Longfellow, I think. Yes. It is not particularly well said, and if I were a fashionable woman I should laugh at it ; but I incline to think it is true'—a remark which, made concerning Lord and Lady Grenvers, had taken a different channel in the girl's thought, and occupied her mind and heart for a considerable part of the journey. She also thought it true.

Something of that fruit-like quality, distinguished in relation of her beauty, there was in Waldine's soul, if one might so distinguish it. She had a healthy soul, not a morbid or starved soul; but its very ripeness was its danger. The touch that impressed it bruised it. It was like a peach without a stone. Mrs. Lupton had the soul of a walnut, riddled and wrinkled with impressions which only went towards its hardening and its flavour; while Lady Grenvers' soul (very deep down indeed) was like the pip of a pear. With Waldine as yet, perhaps always a little, soul and body were indiscriminate and interchangeable. Touch with her meant thought, and utterance followed hard on impulse. Hardly could she feel things mentally which did not reach her through the body—contrariwise when her mind was moved the body flushed or shivered. Love had reached her through the senses, not through the convictions; but the senses influenced her thoughts till they were mere strings of Love's lute. The hours which immediately succeeded John Lyne's first kiss—whether waking or sleeping hours—were literally love-laden ; the animation of her mind was suspended and her every movement listless and relaxed. Body and soul became twin servitors of sense.

And when she had, to some extent, recovered tone, she found she was a different woman. New sympathies were awakened in her, not finer alone, but wider of scope than the old ones, and they were all at present under the dominion of the one absorbing interest. The love of this girl became at once not only a full-grown passion, but her entire self. What was done with her she did not greatly care. They might take her away to London or elsewhere ; she had never been hardly used, and she could not understand disappointment or deprivation ; she had found and appropriated a new life wholly hers ; she had no misgivings. No doubt it was partly youth that made her take things so easily and so contentedly pursue the inexpedient. She was unconscious, to some degree, of the way of the world; she was sufficiently conscious of it to take a pleasure in defying it—that was all. To write expansively and glory in sending the letter fully signed—this was the first result of the new influences. Had she stopped to analyse her mental condition, as at other times she was fond of doing, she might have made the discovery that she went near to rejoicing at the separation which gave her an opportunity of writing so fully and so decisively. But at this extreme of sensation she analysed nothing; she only acted or was inactive as her new self moved her. Mrs. Lupton, who, to her own never-ending regret, always had her emotions thoroughly in hand however much she pretended to let them go, could not have understood Waldine's state had its manifestations been evident. If she could have understood it she would not have rested till she had tried to attain to it and broken her heart at finding it eternally elusive to such a nature as hers. Thus, with the best or the worst of inten-

tions, she could never prove a thorough friend
to Val.

But at least she could amuse her. London
to Mrs. Lupton, at all events out of the season,
was not the treadmill of routine. It was a
Pandora's box, perhaps of evils, certainly of
pleasures, out of which she caught the flying
moments without saying 'stay' to any one of
them. To have an immense fund of occupa-
tions for choice, and then, often enough, to
choose none of them but something entirely
different, was Mrs. Lupton's notion of the
freedom of will in London or Paris. She
could not behave thus to the limited and
formal county engagements, with which her
Netherfield sojourn was starred.

'Something for every half-hour of the day,'
she often said, 'I like to feel *that*, in the morn-
ings : I like to have my little "scheme" that
proves to me that there is no moment from
morning to night when somebody does not particularly wish to see me. And then I like for
some one to come in—perhaps a stranger, perhaps an old friend (I think *preferably* a stranger)

—with something that is scarcely a plan to propose—a stroll in Kensington Gardens, a visit to a studio—some one with just the influence of the moment upon him'—(Mrs. Lupton was great upon the influence of the moment)—'How gladly one throws over all the scheme, lightens the ship of all the ballast and then, *vogue la galère! ce que c'est que d'être femme!*'

'But suppose it is not "him"?' an impertinent friend would argue, with more common sense than grammar—'suppose it is some tiresome bore from the country or some exacting dressmaker, who puts out your day. The sacrifice of your little "scheme" is not so charming then, is it?'

'Oh, "suppose and suppose." . . . My dear, one is a conscious actress, not a puppet. And besides, even then, you have the satisfaction of disappointing the people who expect you. That is *always* delightful,—with the one drawback that you don't see it. But it is at least pleasure enough to give zest to your unpremeditated hours. Then there is the deeper question,

which torments me for ever. Are not the bore
and the dressmaker a pleasure? No : I *don't*
mean "mayn't they be more endurable than one
anticipated?" I mean something more recon-
dite—something "quite horridly blue," as poor
Ethelinda Grenvers says. I mean, Are not
"being bored" and "being tortured" *pleasures?*
are not vexations and disappointments
pleasures? And not only because of one's
sense of martyrdom, but just simply because
they call on one's nerves in an unexpected
way. Are not grief and pain pleasures?—it
is just a system of nomenclature—would not
one far sooner lose one's palate for sweets and
one's taste for pretty things than lose great
griefs, great loves, great agonies out of one's
life? The proof?—the proof is this: the things
we seek, the things after which we greatly strive,
are they not more akin to loss and death than
to amusement? With all my fondness for bon-
bons and theatres, I have got more pleasure out
of a passionate and unrequited love or a cold
midnight vigil by a sick friend—consciously
tasted more nervous satisfaction—than out of

the finest play ever written or the divinest
dishes ever seasoned—*à propos* of which these
chocolates are something new, bitter not sweet,
you will like them.'

Had Mrs Lupton held forth in this strain to
Waldine de Stair, the girl, full to the brim of a
joy which was mere delight, would have replied,
' But you would not call giving pain a pleasure?
surely this pleasure is only a poor spurious sort
of pleasure *malgré* the pain it gives?'

Whereto finally Mrs. Lupton would have
replied, 'My dear Val, one talks lightly and
glibly about giving pain and giving pleasure
—what does one know? What does one
predicate? it is all a habit of speech. One can
only accept intentions. A man gives me a
dog for a plaything : I hate pet dogs, and this
one bites me. But if I could nurse the same
man through an illness I should experience
great pleasure. I may be odd in expressing
myself so frankly. If I were to say I would
rather have opportunities of doing good than
a kingdom, you would approve me, though you
might think me a prig. But when I say I had

far rather a friend of mine had a fever than that he should give me a lap-dog, you look as if I blasphemed. But it is all one :—I have seen pious women rejoice over what they call a reclaimed sheep, and I have seen them weep over an unregenerate death-bed ; and I know perfectly well that the death-bed has been the more real pleasure. Small blame to them ; it excites one more.'

And thus, after reducing all pleasure to excitement and eliminating all tenderness from life, Mrs. Lupton would plume herself on being the one woman in London who had the courage of her opinions. She was, moreover, at this juncture, the one woman in London whose companionship was likely to be poison to Waldine de Stair.

For companions they became, although Waldine, partly from Mrs. Lupton's effusiveness, never had any inclination to make a confidante of her with respect to John Lyne. It was not fear of her hostess that prevented her, so much as reverence for her own deep feeling which she did not now confide to her most intimate correspondent in Brussels.

Moreover the days were full. Although every one they met expressed surprise at seeing Mrs. Lupton, the number of surprised people was so considerable that it was obvious they were not quite unfashionable in their locale. They breakfasted late, and from twelve to two they drove hither and thither to shops and picture-galleries—the latter being the usual trysting-place for some one or other of Mrs. Lupton's artistic swains. To Waldine, with her keen love of colour, it was an *incanto*, after an hour of tedious shopping, to sit quietly in Whistler's brown and yellow gallery and listen to the soft undercurrent of criticism, not unmixed with scandal, upon which Mrs. Lupton loved to set her fancies afloat. Then after luncheon in Curzon Street or, with other birds of passage, at hotels or great houses half shut up, where some cosy nook had been brightened for the hostess in her flying visit, they would drive out again to studios or teas less formal than the season's, where there was whatever music might be available of the best. Then there were dinners, not too late for the theatres

to which they never went alone ; and occasion-
ally evenings when they dined out or had friends
with them, generally all going on together to
some large party, artistic and musical, which
would bring them well into the following
morning.

A year before, the girl would have enjoyed
the varied monotony of this pleasant London
life with avidity ; but now it seemed to her
not to be stirring, at all, or anything more than
faintly amusing. She had been so deeply
moved that for some weeks she would be able
to take part in the pageant of this existence
without its impressing or fatiguing her in the
least.   And this listlessness gave her beauty a
strange charm in contrast to Mrs. Lupton's
brightness and *insouciance* of quite a different
order.   Val's listlessness was not impertinence
—like Mrs. Lupton's—it was merely a phase
of preoccupation.   In the cold nervous weather
her clear warm pallor and shining serious eyes
were provokingly attractive.   And she was
never sad enough to be dull.   The wine of
life which those first kisses had poured into

her veins, intoxicated her still. She was seldom at a loss for an answer, though she was very often inattentive. If the thought of John became too much for silence, she wrote to him.

One evening, when they had been dining at the Bachelors' Club and were just crossing the long landing before descending to their carriage, they encountered Mr. Launcelot Denham: one of the two young men who were their hosts and who were going on with them to the French plays, was a cousin of his, and it was his familiar greeting on the stairs which made Waldine turn those serious eyes of hers in Mr. Denham's direction.

'Oh Launce!' said Mrs. Lupton, who was never surprised, 'are you a "bachelor"? Look, I have put my hook into your cousin's nose: you must come with us and protect him.'

'Come where?' said the Hon. Launcelot, stifling an unholy aspiration for Opéra Bouffe.

'To the French plays. I'm sure you'll like them,—they're very improper.'

'But I shan't understand them, and I haven't got a stall.'

' I will explain them as far as my compre-
hension serves, and you can draw on your
imagination for the rest. You can get a place
at the theatre and come and sit with us. If
you have your hansom you can take Lord
Lexford ; we had much rather be three in the
brougham than four, and you can have your
talk out there. Lex, dear, your room is really
better than your company on that small back
seat,—Helbert's legs are shorter.'

Mr. Denham, not yet wholly freed from that
heathenish hankering after comic songs and
dances, glanced at Waldine de Stair, while Mrs.
Lupton glibly arranged his transit.

' Yes !' she said with a little smile, ' come
with us, *Monsieur de l'argent :* you are so fond
of French, I remember.'

She was glad to see him : he was fresh
from Netherfield, and on the big light staircase of the club he seemed to summon up a
country breeze—his bright hair, as he stood
before her with uncovered head, reminded her
of the autumn leaves at Whiteknyghts. She
felt to breathe the influences native to John

Lyne, beholding Launcelot Denham. 'Yes, come with us,' she said, and, as if the persuasion in her tone were not enough, she smiled. Who can blame him that he read the augury of her smile as kind?

The French comedies proved rather dull, but Mrs. Lupton's box was deep enough for the party to converse unheard, and the Hon. Launcelot ceased altogether to regret puns and dances when his hostess bade him return with them to Curzon Street for some supper before he went back to his room in St. James'. It was not often that Mrs. Lupton put herself out so far as to offer supper even to her 'second selves,' but when she did it was of the best, and a thing to be remembered.

It was during the evening only that she bethought her of the invitation, but she managed to scribble a line to her housekeeper, and get it entrusted to a commissionaire. The result was that when the brougham and hansom reached Mayfair a charming little banquet was prepared in the small front room where she dined, out of the season. It was a luxurious *bonbonnière* of an apartment, fitted with plush couches and hangings of a shade half copper and half crimson—a kind of Indian red which was equally becoming to her own pertness and Waldine's beauty. There was a small round table, lit by an elaborate hanging-lamp of bronze and brass—from Mrs. Lupton's own design (filtered out of Mr. Collington's pencil)— the light from which, tempered by festoons of brick dust silk, fell upon dishes of aspic and fruit and the silver covers of hot soup and cutlets. There were no flowers on the table, but a large blue bowl of Christmas roses was, with a few screens of peacocks' feathers, the only adornment of the broad chimney-piece, which, like the rest of the furniture, was of white wood.

There was nothing vulgar in the aspect of the little supper gleaming on the white damask. Perfect of its kind, it was at the same time absolutely unpretentious. It looked like something to eat, not like something to stare at or to smell. And the white walls, the deep-toned hangings, the shaded but untinted lights, as well as the delicate fare, were admirable adjuncts to Mrs. Lupton's prismatic toilette and Waldine's simple dress of ivory silk. The two young lordlings—Lexford and Helbert—felt themselves in favour, while Denham was quite solemnised with happiness. The sight of the piled-up mantles on the sofa—Mrs. Lupton's furs and satin-lined velvet cloak, and Waldine's white wrappings and long seal overcoat—filled the young man's senses with a new strange pleasure. He thought of Opéra Bouffe without a sigh, he thought of bachelor quarters and regretted their discomfort. He was not of the order of modern manhood which busies itself with the decoration of its chambers.

'Your silence is quite *tomb-y*, Launce,' said Mrs. Lupton as she unwound her fair cropped head from its last lace scarf:—'You are a skeleton at my little feast—fleshy, but still, to the philosophic eye, a skeleton.'

'Oh no!' said the Hon. Launcelot rather pointlessly, and the blank stupidity of his answer told Mrs. Lupton something of what was in his heart. She followed the direction of his eyes, which rested upon Waldine's form as she too put off the endless yards of lace with which her cream - white throat was swathed.

'This is nicer than the theatre,' she said in a soft full voice, as she came up to the fire. The cold night had paled her face, but her arms were like warm satin, from the protection of the seal-skin coat. They were so beautiful and so expressive of her youth and sex that Mr. Denham's face flushed as she ungloved them : he was very susceptible.

'Do you never wear bracelets ?' he said.

'Never,' said Waldine. 'I hate trinkets, I look at jewellers' shops and wonder who can buy those cases full of rubbish in the windows. If I had Mrs. Lupton's diamonds I might wear them—*pas autrement.*'

The Hon. Launcelot, who had in his breast-pocket one of the said morocco cases, the contents of which he had taken half the afternoon to select at Streeter's for one of the young ladies who nightly murdered her part in the Opéra Bouffe, was rather astonished at this new departure. His notion had been that all girls liked bangles and brooches.

'You are so different to every one else,' he said reflectively; and though the remark was ambiguous, the tone conveyed a compliment.

'I *am* odd,' said Waldine, sitting down in a chair of gilt carved wood with ornaments and arms of the ruby plush :—'Give me one of those peacock screens: I don't want to be ugly as well.'

She was so wholly careless of his feelings that she did not in the least mind what opportunities for pretty speeches she gave him, and his feeling for her was too honest and too shy for him to take full advantage of them. He gave her the screen, with which she fanned herself slowly. One little curl on her left temple waved to and fro with the air it made: he felt as if his senses came and went with the sway of that little curl.

'Make Lord Helbert come and give me his opinion of my new mantelpiece in the hall, Lex,' said Mrs. Lupton to Lord Lexford :—'It is not often one can secure the verdict of such

a judge before it is too late. And the thing
is only half done, so that if he suggests anything I can introduce it.'

'Tell me about Netherfield,' said Waldine,
when they were alone, still fanning herself
at the same pace, as she leaned back in her
chair.

'Lord Grenvers is awfully ill,' said Mr.
Denham sympathetically, stirring the bright
wood-fire with his foot, where he stood by the
hearth.

'That I know. He is like Mother Hub-
bard's dog!'

'Her ladyship sees nobody except—but that
is scandal!'

'What is scandal? my aunt is above all
scandal.'

'Of course she is really : only I'm so jealous
because she won't see *me*, you know.'

'Whom does she see?'

'Only that lucky fellow Lyne. The way
they spoil him is absurd.'

—(No answer, and the pace of the waved
fan unchanged.)—

'They treat him more like a son than a
bailiff: he is always with his lordship, and
she gives him tea in her boudoir. He's been
ill or something'—

—(The fan stops waving, but Val does not
speak: surely, where the want of the heart to
hear something is so intense, there can be no
need of questions.)—

'Got cold after Mrs. Lupton's tableaux,
walking home or some folly. And then pleurisy
—but he's all right again now.'

—(The fan begins waving afresh, more
slowly but in little nervous jerks.)—

'Bad thing, pleurisy.'

'Is it?'

'Rather: carried off my poor mother—
awful loss to a chap that is, Miss de Stair.'

Waldine put down the fan. The expression
of her face was singularly wistful and gentle:
one would almost imagine tears behind the
long, dark lashes. Evidently, thought her devoted swain, she is not quite indifferent to
what grieves or moves me.

He proceeded to improve the occasion.

'Yes : I always feel that there's nothing to make up for it at home now. There's only one sort of thing that can console a fellow, you know——' he hesitated.

'And that is ?' said Waldine absently.

'Supper,' said Mrs. Lupton, at this instant, reappearing with Lords Lexford and Helbert.

CHAPTER III.

AT WHITEKNYGHTS

AMONG the many surprises familiar to our capricious England is that of an April day in the latter half of December. Often after three stern white frosts it breathes in dawn over the land, half promise and half regret. 'Do not forget me,' says past summer, looking back; 'I am coming,' says spring, looking forward: it is like the kiss of both. Just such a morning befell the country within a week of Christmas, and became Whiteknyghts bravely. It was as if nature stretched herself, with thawed limbs, out of her winter sleep. The breath of the day was like the breathing of a warm creature over the slushy roads and cold pools. The grass put off its white mantle

and showed in a great plain of wide untroubled
green where, every now and then, an elfin
shred of the sapless bracken looked like the
ghost of a robin. All sorts of unimagined
plants appeared in view amid relics of de-
parted autumn. Nature would turn to sleep
again under her whitening coverlet, the little
growing roots and the poor sodden relics
would disappear. This was just a moment of
youth in age, of maturity in innocence ; but
it was a moment irresistible in its charm.
The deed that suggested itself on such a
morning one would do, as it were under the
spell of a dream.

What suggested itself to John Lyne was to
superintend the ordering of part of a planta-
tion, which, being visible from his usual
sitting - room, was Lord Grenvers' peculiar
care. Fresh shrubs were being planted in
among too scattered trees, while crowded
undergrowth in other places was making way
for unguessed vistas of view. Landscape
gardening was not properly in John's province, but he knew what Lord Grenvers

wished to see and what he wished to have hidden, and his taste was as much to be trusted as his discretion. Moreover there had been a talk of sacrificing Miss de Stair's ash-tree, which chanced to be parallel with a fine oak from one point of observation, and this ash-tree—which had become the most sacred of the Whiteknyghts wood in his eyes—he was resolved to spare. So there he was among the labourers, on this fantastic winter day which was as warm as summer, his brown and white plaid coat thrown open over his knitted waistcoat and his tan gaiters splashed with earth and leaves. No companionship and no costume could have brought out so strikingly his conspicuous refinement of look.

This was, perhaps, intensified by the severe illness through which he had passed, of which Mr. Denham had made cursory mention to Waldine at Mrs. Lupton's. John's difference to his compeers was not one of aspect only, it was unluckily one of constitution also, and on the burning excitement of the tableaux and their sequel his long walk homewards through the icy night had induced a chill which had attacked his hitherto unfevered lungs. For some days he had been suffering from a cough, which seemed to have left him wholly for the first time to-day under the healing of the balmy air. This morning he looked renewed and refreshed, the better—not the worse—for his illness. And it was pleasant to him to inhale the rare soft breeze, just flavoured by the smoke which rose thin and blue from a smouldering heap of twigs and leaves where the woodmen had made their fire. It is not like labour, this easy outdoor work ; it is like the native play of Adam's sons.

An exquisite laziness stole over John's limbs at midday, when his subordinates were grouped about their dinner—half it was the unwonted weakness of returning health and half the influences of the quiet day—a laziness careless and buoyant. He turned from the still scene, where axe and chopper were hushed for an hour, and with a smile upon his lips strolled in the direction of the beloved tree.

His eyes were cast down on the unveiled

land, which he was not, like most of his kind,
too stupid to observe. They rested happily
upon the ferns, the bits of dark brown brier
and the variegated ivy which he was glad to
see again after their white burial. These
grew at either side his way, but his immediate
footprints were on a track which was almost
worn into a path by now. It went—the least
bit out of his way home, be it confessed—to
Waldine's ash-tree, which with its twin stems
was more noticeable than before amid the
general leaflessness of the scene ; soon after,
joining a road which branched two ways—the
right-hand turn leading to John's home, the
left in the direction of Mrs. Lupton's forsaken
halls. Where the path joined the road there
was a stile, and when John Lyne reached this
stile it was just half-past twelve o'clock on
this December day. Netherfield church clock
was striking.

There was no hurry—John's dinner-hour
was one, but he was not tied to it because it
happened that both his parents were away.
They had not gone far, only down to Nether-

field to make their small preparations for the
Christmas season; but, being both in years,
they would honour appreciative connections
in the town with their presence to dinner,
when the marketing was done, so as to get a
good rest and chat before John drove down to
fetch them at dusk. Thus he was obliged to
keep near home, having the key of the house
in his pocket, but free to choose his own
moment for the frugal meal that awaited him
there. And this moment was not now; the
stile—quite dry in the noonday sun—was too
tempting; he climbed up and sat down, with
his pensive eyes still on the ash-tree and his
back to the road.

Presently he lit his pipe, and the touch of
his pocket-book to his hand, as he did so,
would have reminded him of Waldine if he
had ever forgotten her for a single instant.
He drew out her last letter and he read these
words from the close of it:

'I am getting sorry that I told you not to
write: if I do not hear of you I shall begin to
think you are only a misty phantom of the

meadows : I shall cease to believe you real.
But that is not what I most fear. Indeed I
have no sort of fears that you are not true.
My fear is that I shall become unreal myself :
my fear is that I shall forget you.—In that case
what would become of me, what should I do ?'

He did not understand the cry of the heart
which spoke in those words. The effort
against evaporation under many-sided pressure
was an effort of which he had no experience.
For him to forget was impossible. He loved
deeply : he had striven against his love until
he had the certainty that it was an accepted
thing ; then he became one with it, the flame
of it the flame of his life. He was hers, she
was his. The first was easy, the second
difficult ; but both were truths. 'Forget?'
he did not understand.

He sat and pondered, still as some woodland
creature in the crystal morning. With his russet
clothes, the rooks might have taken him for part
of the landscape, but for the little waft of smoke
from his pipe at steady intervals ; their sentinel
sat on a bough and watched him ; perhaps the

bird would have understood light love better. To meet, to pair, to part. No; John would never come to think that this was love. Waldine's letters were marvels to him, sacred marvels which were his dearest possession. There was nothing that she said, in her fluent, exuberant moods, which his heart did not echo steadfastly ; he had got used to let her flute-stops express the song of his heart, and the piping which was her satisfaction taught his love a tune ; but in this last movement of the music he had no skill to join. 'My fear is that I shall become unreal myself.' Here was perplexity indeed. What was the world doing? he did not know.

So silent he was that a traveller might have passed him by, and so absorbed in thought that he did not hear a footstep which came softly brushing through the hedgerow grass. Nearer and nearer it came, light as the step of a girl who nears her heart's desire. And when it stopped close by him—suddenly and short—it was no more than if the air drops, less than if a leaf rustles.

'Are you not real, Waldine de Stair?' he said aloud in his grave and tender tone.

'I am quite real, John Lyne, and I am here,' said an answering voice behind him.

It was she indeed; her shadow almost fell upon the letter in his hand. In a second he had turned and faced her with that sort of light in his whole look that mountains catch at sunrise. She was standing on the grassy edge of the road, half shy, half bold, an incarnation of beauty and love. Her lips and eyes were like jewels in the softness of her fair and wind-fanned face.

'Why don't you speak to me?' she said at last, laughing softly for joy.

For although he said no word to her as yet, there was no doubt of his welcome. . . . How kind and liberal was this winter day! were there ever any two hearts so utterly and unreservedly and happily alone?

The stile was still between them. 'Don't come across to me,' she said in breathless gasps, 'I want to see you there: it is too good to be true! Listen, John. I have come all this

way to find you : I must tell you at once before I am afraid of you, while I still feel as if
it were only the king of dreams that I speak
to. I could not do without you any longer.
No one knows I am come. . . . Oh! do not
look at me. . . . I am ashamed, I don't
know why '— and breaking off from speech,
she suddenly wheeled round and buried her
face in her fur muff.

John stood quite still : his heart beat in
his chest like a sledge hammer : it was with
difficulty that he found words, when he did
they came slowly and low : 'Oh,' he said,
'you are not dead? you are my own sweet
love? . . . and welcome.'

With his utterance a sort of trembling
seemed to shake her : in a second he had strode
across the stile, and his warm arms were round
her. But her courage was gone. She hid
her burning face upon his shoulder, and a
quick string of nervous speech escaped her
lips.

'I cannot tell you what it was—Mrs. Lupton went on a journey—I was alone : I had

driven with her to the station in a cab, it was
too early for the carriage. . . . I told the footman something—I don't know what—because
I saw there was a train just starting—I took a
ticket—I got in—I walked from the station.'

'Have you done right, have you run any
risks ?'

'I did not like to come on to Netherfield,
I got out at Mrs. Lupton's station : no one
knew me. I walked . . . it did not seem
far . . . and then I saw you.'

'Thank God. What if you had not seen
me ?'

'*I should have died—I should have gone
on and seen my aunt.*'

The instantaneous contradiction was so
artless that they both laughed—that double
ripple of laughter, deep with sweet, than which
there is no better music.

'Do not laugh, John—listen ! think what
I have done. I have found you and I have
two hours. Have you two hours which you
will give me for mine ?'

'I have better than that: I have all my life.'

'*Soit!* but just now it is these two hours
that I want. John, have you a well-regulated
mind?'

'Not just now.'

'No, but presently; because I will tell you
a secret, "I am tired:" that sounds all right;
but the rest sounds horrible, "I am hungry."
I thought when I had found you I should not
feel hungry, but I do. Is food possible?'

'Listen to *me* now!'—He spoke as one
speaks to a child, but his voice quivered :—
'I am all alone at home to-day. Only two
hundred yards away from here there is a house
and a fire and food . . . and a welcome. But
you will go on to the Court.'

'Do you think so? Oh! my king of
dreams, before you grow too dreadfully real,
let me tell you that a fireless barn with your
welcome and a crust of bread—only just now
I'm very particular about that crust of bread—
is better to me than all the Courts in Europe.
And no, John, no! I am not going to be sent
on to my people. If you are alone like this,
it is Providence, and we "must not fly in the

face of" Aunt Ethelinda's favourite Providence.
For these two hours let us forget the world.'

'With all my heart,' said John Lyne, 'your
world we will forget, but you are all my world.'

'Very well—that is understoood.   Now
listen to me,'—she pushed him from her a little,
and looked at him with her glowing eyes,—
'Answer me quick and straight : do you love
me ?'

'You only, you ever; so help me God,'
said John.

'I wanted to hear you say it : I am sure of
you now.   Say "yes" three times.'

'Yes—yes—yes.'

'The first "yes" is this : you will never
breathe my coming.   The second "yes" is
this : you are mine for these two hours.   The
third "yes" is this : when I am gone you will
forget that I have been here—forget it wholly
and for ever.'

'Why don't you command me things that
matter for always.   Why so set on *now?*'

'Because it *is* now that matters for always.
People are so full of long promises and great

hopes. I hate them both. I want and I claim to-day—to-day and you.'

' They are both yours, my darling. . . .'

Then silence, just because no word was sweet enough for speech. . . .

After a moment— ' Then, John,' she said, ' I will tell you what I will do with my gifts. I will use the one for the other: let me help you in your daily life. Tell me things to do.'

' To-day is holiday : if you will please me you will come and dine : home is close by.'

' I am not tired. This moment I thought I was, but now, " my heart is full of rest." '

She did not look tired: she looked like some radiant creation of sunbeams in the vigour and freshness of her lovely youth. And the sunbeams seemed spilt also over her shining furs.

Her broken sentences had told John all he needed to know: more plainly the facts were these : Mrs. Lupton had been for some time in treaty for a villa on the sea-coast, the purchase of which was just completed. Unkind rumour—which she made a point of encouraging—affirmed that her frequent visits to it were not made alone. On this particular day she was due there to arrange some final preliminaries as to its alteration and—to tell for her, first, what she would not have concealed —she was going to install Mr. Collington there to superintend the decorations of the drawing-room. There was no need to take Waldine. If her trip shocked the girl, so much the better : it would be a pity if she discovered that the talk was wholly of " apple greens " and " French grays "—Mrs. Lupton would lose the *prestige* of her flirtations : she made a little mystery of the journey to Val.

'You shall come and see me off at the station, and meet me in the evening. I have ordered the carriage at seven ;' she had said. ' Amuse yourself well and lunch where you will.'

As her train steamed out of the station Waldine had recognised the platform as that of the Netherfield line. It was early, little past nine o'clock, and she chanced to remember the time-table. There was an express just

starting which would bring her to Netherfield
in less than three hours. To tell the young
footman that she would not want him—that
she had to meet a friend with whom she
would spend the day—was the work of a
moment. In three minutes she had got her
ticket, and in a minute more had found an
untroubled solitude in a railway carriage.
The 3.15 train back would land her at the
station in town by half-past six, so that, as
Mrs. Lupton's train was not timed to arrive
till 7.5, she could await her hostess in the
brougham. Waldine's impulsiveness and
innocence together compounded for her a
strange independence which was one of her
most dangerous and fascinating traits. The
glow of it kept her from any conscience-chills in
her extraordinary proceeding, while it quickened her inventive faculties: she determined
to get out at the little station which Mrs.
Lupton used, where she would be taken for
one of that lady's many erratic visitors, who
came and went pretty much as they liked
during her own absence. At Netherfield

Whiteknyghts was all; but county boundaries are strongly marked, and at the next station, only three miles off, Whiteknyghts was nothing.

The bright soft air of the exhilarating day was like a tonic to the girl's nerves, and it was not till she came close to John Lyne's house that she felt her heart sink; there then commenced in her spirits a reaction which would have overwhelmed her, and very likely sent her on to her aunt with some excuse of home-sickness, had she not come upon the object of her quest and heard his spoken words. To answer them aloud was irresistible, and she found herself launched once more upon the tide of passion whereon she floated thus serenely.

They walked on down the lane, which was so hedged with evergreen and fir that it wore a summer aspect quite in harmony with the day's; and away to their right Waldine remarked the thin blue smoke which rose from the woodmen's noontide fire. There was something strangely pleasant to the lovers in this sign of life so near them and yet so

remote; it was a sort of suggestion how fickle
was the tenure of these stolen moments, which
trebled their sweetness. But they were quite
secure; not until much later in the day would
some market-woman pass up this road, and
probably the wheels of John's cart when he
went to fetch his parents would be the first
sound upon the sylvan silence. Two hours of
solitude, mutual and undisturbed, were to
be their portion.

'My scheme is this,' said Waldine, as they
approached the little house, which, despite
all her plans, she had never visited :—' We will
play at being old friends : suppose now, John,
that you have been at work all the morning, and
I have been at home preparing your dinner.'

'Then we shall have to suppose you have
prepared a very poor one.'

'Never mind that. "Better is a dinner
of herbs——"'

'"Where love is,"' added John, empha-
sising the quotation by taking her hand—

'"Than a stalled ox and hatred withal,"'
she concluded briskly, withdrawing it.

He took his latchkey from his pocket, and Waldine laughed at it because it was so clumsy and old-fashioned—such a contrast to the London latchkey which Mrs. Lupton aired so daintily and was for ever leaving at home. As they passed together up the garden-path, she took it from him that she might unlock the door herself.

'Welcome home,' said John, as they stood together on the threshold. There was a late rose growing under the shelter of the porch; he had watched it for some days; he stooped and picked it now.

CHAPTER IV.

AT HOME

THERE is nothing mean in the configuration of John Lyne's abode. It has a certain old-fashioned simplicity which lets it hold its own even in comparison with Mrs. Lupton's gilded halls. Here all is Spartan, but the severity is symmetrical and the effect of it refined. Ugly things there are—the gauze protected looking-glass, the antimacassar-shrouded chairs, the beadwork mats—but they have a trivial air; they do not greatly offend because they are palpably ephemeral—a touch would sweep them away: what is permanent is the fine old crust of the quaint house; the sun that lights it, the breeze that airs it, these endure and recur—a quarter of an hour would rid the rooms of all traces of a past hundred years, another quarter of an hour would reinstate them wholly. The simple, solid house, where generations have been born, have led their honest lives and died, it is never without dignity; in this case it is not entirely without beauty. And Waldine has of late been too spoiled to be critical; the mood of her journey is protest—reaction; if her lover lived in a cottage she would be satisfied and glad. The character of the house being, to a certain extent, the character of its inmates, one is led to conjecture, not amiss, that looking-glasses, antimacassars, and beadwork mats have been presents—tributes of respect to John Lyne's mother and grand-mother—when one sees the meal that is ready for his return. It is plain, homely fare, but it is set out with a neatness which makes it appetising. There is cold meat and ham; there is some vegetable soup in a pot over the fire, and there is cold plum-pudding, for which Waldine has a school-girl's passion. The butter and the bread are perfect, being indeed the same that are supplied to White-knyghts; and there is home-made wine in a carved corner-cupboard underneath the clock, which seems to tick out loudly, 'Look up, look up,' as if insisting that no moment of the precious hours should be lost.

Her survey of the parlour has resulted in Waldine's opening John's little piano which occupies the place of honour there and has attracted her attention; but it is with the larger room—half dining-hall, half kitchen—that she is most enchanted. In the gay light, which it is impossible to believe the same that struggles through the murk of a London fog, each old bit of furniture seems to laugh and shine—the place to its farthest crevice seems aware of the lovely and unwonted presence for which it must put on its finest smile. The seal-skin of the girl's Parisian coat is not more glossy than the old oak settle upon which she throws it, the satin lining of her muff is dull beneath the brightness of the old brass warming-pan above it. But her beauty holds its own, it pales the sunlight and the fire. She flits hither and thither like a foreign bird in a barn, and wherever she rests for a moment, the eye recalls her grace. She is perfume, laughter, music, warmth, delight—love. John Lyne has hung up his cap in the hall, and he stands—dazed with pleasure—watching her explore his ancient home. He forgets that it is himself whom she has come to see; he is unconscious of the possessive charm of his own presence; it seems to him as if she were come to be a glory on each old familiar thing, which shall be no more as it was when her sojourn is over. But to be indoors sets off his stature and his face, and there is no discrepance in his dress with the apparatus of his simple home. Even his tan boots are in keeping on the stone floor, and there is nothing that the sunshine touches to such beauty as his curly hair. The genius of the place, it is he that really satisfies the girl's heart with this unknown, unequalled thrill of soft content. It is he that is the prize of her seeking.

Half wilful and half shy, she does not look

at him now; and he is so chivalrous, so reverent, that he lets her take her own way, neither by speech nor glance embarrassing her or making her feel that there is any danger or scandal in her scheme. He lends himself to her charming will with his easy, loyal nature. He neither helps nor hinders her actions; his attitude says plainly, 'All that I have and all that I am are yours.' The treatment of her chattels, that is for her to decide, who is the lady of his homestead and the mistress of his life.

Her decision is favourable to both. She is bent upon beneficence—and luncheon! She throws two sheep-skin mats beneath the little table where the board is partly spread; she signs to John to draw up two arm-chairs, instead of the straight, high-backed pair which are set for Mr. and Mrs. Lyne in their places against the wall. In an instant she has given a touch of luxury and ease to the little banquet. And this, too, she will serve in her own way. 'We must garnish our soup,' she says laughing, and flings open the corner cupboard where Mrs. Lyne's sauces are ranged.

'Chili vinegar! John, it is what his lord-ship always takes in soup; get it out. How I wish I could cook! But I *can* make a salad,'—and she sets to work with some fresh vegetables.

She has turned up her neat sleeves over the rounded wrists; and John Lyne marks, as Launcelot Denham marked in London, the beauty of her girlish arms. But he does not contemplate them as Mr. Denham took leave to do. Her beauty will recur to him when this sunny day is done, haunting his senses like a fever. The oval shape of her slim waist, the firmness of her graceful shoulders to which the plain gown clings so lovingly, they will have due place in the recollected image that will fill his dreams; but *not* to take her in his arms, *not* to tell her what is in his heart—that is the effort now. When she stoops close to him, and, raising up her head, lets the fragrance of her hair reach him; when she touches him lightly in passing, when her laughter fans towards him the pure warmth of her breath—at every moment of contact, at all proximity—there is built within his brain, ever deeper and ever dearer, the face and figure of his idol. His passion, restrained though he keeps it, is like a cumulative poison which makes gradual headway in his veins because of her exceeding loveliness and charm. He is glad with a great joy that is like the revelation of bliss undreamed and unimagined pleasure. He is in fairyland; the caprice of his fancy is realised beyond its utmost conception.

To the caprice of *her* fancy there is no limit but that of time and space; she has no such bounded routine as has been his, to circumscribe her horizon. His eight and twenty years of sameness find no parallel in her nineteen, so lightly lived amid various changes of scene and company. To sit in twilight and become suddenly possessed of the sun, that would be a surprise; but to find one's self an inhabitant of the sun after a series of short stays on planets at will, would be little more than a halting-stage in a journey.

'I am famished! come and eat.'

They seat themselves and taste their mutual meal. Waldine is honestly hungry, and though she has but the appetite of a healthy bird, she makes a feint at least of eating her luncheon. John cannot eat. There is a sort of hurry in his nature which will not let him feed it. Unpractised nerves of sense are at their utmost tension, the demands of usual fibres are forgotten. She does not notice his abstinence. Her delicate organisation recruits itself quickly; the soup and meat which she tastes, sitting at rest in the warm bright room, strengthen her to banish fatigue and shyness. She is at home; she feels as if she lived in that room and ate at that table always. The strangeness that abides is his, in his own house, not hers.

'To me this is the happy life,' she says, with that perception of her pleasure while she enjoys it which is so rare and which doubles the value of existence. 'I don't know how you live or what you do, but I feel as if I knew it all. You will have to see after those woodmen, *ami* John, and I shall prepare your tea; and then we shall play and sing all through the winter evening, shutting out the tiresome world with those good strong shutters; is not that so? Ah no! I shall be dining in London and you will be walking through the dark to Whiteknyghts. I think I am jealous of some one who is at Whiteknyghts.'

'There *was* some one there that I love,' says John, humouring her with a smile, 'but she went away to London and forgot me.'

'For a time.' Her eyes look very long and tender in the clear afternoon light; she sits facing it with the frank carelessness of her beauty. 'No; I am not jealous of that girl, John, I think I am jealous of my aunt.'

They both laugh.

'By the way, tell me what she says to you.'

'Never a word about *you*. When I came back with the doctor for his lordship you were gone with Mrs. Lupton. Each morning I have met the postman; but I supposed that you could not do that in London, so I hesitated before writing, and then you forbade me.'

'I know ; I hate complications, and I don't care for letters.   I like to write them.'

'Since then I have had a sort of fever, and she has been very kind.'

'You must not have fevers ; I hate illnesses ; and you must not let her be kind.   You are well again now, are you not ?'

'Never better—never half so well.'

'But thinner.   I did not see it in your thicker coat at first.   *Ami* John, do you know that you are very good to look at.'

'So that you are here to see me, I am glad.'

'Eat and drink.   I want to do you good. I heard of your illness ; if I had been nice I should have told you that it was the news of it which brought me.   But it was not.   I wanted to see you, to make sure that you existed.   And if I had found you ill, I should have been angry.   *Sono fatta così.*'

He smiles again, disbelieving her though she is speaking the absolute truth.

—'And now we will make plans.   I do not want to stay away any longer.   No ; I am not really jealous of her ladyship ; I do not care.

But I care to see you. I mean to return and you are to do all that I choose.'

A shadow passes over his face as he listens. ' May I speak first ?' he says decisively.

'If you mean, "may you speak to her ladyship first,"—no. Certainly not. If you mean, " may you say something to me now," —proceed.'

He had meant the former: she has incidentally denied him his request, and it is difficult for him to repeat it in view of her leave that he shall say what he wills to her. He leans across the table, looking very sombre and earnest ; she gazes straight out of the window, only her lips twitch a little and her colour comes and goes.

' Waldine,' he says gravely, ' you mean well by me, do you not ? '

' I don't know what you call well—I love you.'

' That is enough. I will tell you what love means to me. It means all.'

She makes a little comprehensive gesture with her hands, part mocking and part nervous.

He goes on steadily. 'That you should love me in the sense I mean, is so immense a thing that I want you to understand it.'

'I do not want to understand it : *c'est plus fort que moi.*'

There is a shortness in her answer which tells him plainly that she has envisaged the subject and put it by.

'Think of it in all its bearings,' he says, after a pause, 'think what you give up.'

'I give up nothing,' she says quickly, 'I keep all I have and I take you.'

'But is that possible ?'

'"Is it possible?" *ami* John, is it not the case ? I am here with you : what do I lose?— a dull luncheon in London. And *yes!* I know something of what you would say, and I ask you, *de grâce*, not to say it. I think it would spoil my day. You tell me love means all to you. I tell you it means all to me. Is not that enough ? What does it matter if the two "alls" are not exactly the same ?'—and John cannot forbear a smile at her logic, while he has not the heart to contradict her conclusion.

'Therefore,' she proceeds with the air of one who has disposed of a parenthesis, 'my plan is this: we will win Lord Grenvers and my aunt by gradual means. They are devoted to you, and they are too unused to me to mind greatly what I do. We will be nice to them, *ami* John, and they will come round to our point of view. Meanwhile I dream of a second life all the time—a life together, yours and mine—like the birds' life in the fields: this is its commencement, there is nothing to hinder its continuing.'

Still John is silent; she is so plausible, so sure, that he is half ashamed of the warnings of his conscience.

'Ah! do not look at me so critically, one would think I were proposing a crime'—she too leans forward now, and speaks quickly and below her breath. 'Ever since I have been here this has been my dream—a life of friendship with you which should be the song of which my other life, with all its music, should be nothing more than an accompaniment. I think approval would spoil this a little : I want to keep my happiness hidden from all the world. Do you not understand? I want to wake in the morning and think that a mile of woodland lane will bring me to you, that a special hour in the day will be your hour with me. I want contrast in my life : almost I fancy Mrs. Lupton has taught me this want. I should *prefer* to live tiresome days at the Court and know that there would be a moment of this home-feeling in each—*greatly* prefer that to living simply here. Don't look so sad, John. It is not that I do not like you,'—she pauses, and the tears flood her lovely eyes,—' it is because I like you so well. That is the fashion of my soul,'—in an instant the tears have given place to a light smile,— ' the dress I like best, John, the food I prefer, I do not want to wear and eat the same always. I should go on liking them, do not be afraid ; but the delight of expectation and of remembrance, these would be gone.'

' And your love would be less without these.'

' I do not say that : I do not know how

great it is or how much greater it may become.
But I want to foster it in my own way, and
you must spoil me so far. Has my plan no
charm for you?'

'Yes : it has charm.'

'Great changes may occur : how do we
know what may happen? The chances of the
world and life may bring us gradually nearer
without our making efforts. And an effort
might part us beyond our own recall—think
of that, John.'

'Yes, I am afraid that is true.'

'Well, then, it is wisest as well as best that
we should trust each other?'

That little turn of her voice as she questions
him—it is more than he can bear. He rises
abruptly and walks to the window. What is
he to do? Is he to warn her of a danger of
which she never seems to dream? Is it not
more manly, as her host, and more true, as her
lover, for him to accede to her simple plan—
putting his life in her hands, and see that no
harm befalls her in the scheme she proposes—
than to urge her to a final step at once of which

she might repent too late. With himself her
guardian, she can always find safety against him.

She leans back in her chair, radiant, contented, happy. She watches him with a
luxurious sense of pleasure : she has no sort of
notion of the ferment in his brain. She waits
for him to speak without the slightest apprehension ; and though he does not look at her,
he is aware of that sunshiny calm in her heart
which her eyes express.

'Waldine,' he says at last—for the taste of
her name is very sweet to his mouth—'I am
older than you are.'

'Ten years I think,' in the slow untroubled
voice with which a nymph might murmur
singing and swinging on a wave.

'And what I ought to say to you is this:
"Go from me altogether."'

'But that you will not say,' she answers
in the same tone, with no trace of surprise.

'But that I *cannot* say,' he repeats in a low,
hoarse voice—the trouble is all his,—'and
therefore I say this : do with me what you
will, there is nothing in my life but you. I

will be satisfied if I am something at least in
yours.'

'Something, John? are you not all?'

'I think that you think so. Love, I have
no more doubt of you than I have of the light,
but I have a longing that all you have and are
should be the best. Realise what it is that
you hold out to me—all that my heart most
seeks—companionship, understanding, beauty.
And then by and by, if you blame me for
grasping at these, try at least to forgive me.'

'Your voice sounds sad, John, let me see
your face.'

He does not turn towards her yet. 'And
in return,' he goes on in the same low voice,
but firmly, with a vibration in his tone that
thrills her as she listens—'in return for my life
make me one promise. While you meet me,
while you accept my . . . friendship, you will
love but me. You say, and truly, there
come times of change. If change takes hold
of your heart, tell me, and I will put the world
between us and leave you free. I would bear
it if you told me honestly that your love had

died : I would bear it though it broke my heart.
But one thing I could not and I would not
bear—to share you with another. I come of
an old country stock, and we have all of us had
notions of honour which would seem strained
to you. I do not want you to enter into
them, but I want you to know them. Where
we are loved we are faithful to death ; where
we are deceived we kill. It was so once and
it will be so again. We kill or we die—at any
rate there is an end. That is the only stigma
on my family,' he adds, lifting his head more
erect as he names it :—' I have heard it spoken
of with shame, but I am proud of it. . . . You
will not deceive me.'

'I adore you,' says the girl beneath her
breath.

Then he turns his head. The effort it has
been to him to speak has flushed his face and
straightened his posture. His eyes glow and
his handsome mouth is set into a stern smile.
Waldine has not changed her attitude, but her
cheek has paled a little. She has the look of
one who listens to stirring music—her lips are

parted, her eyes dwell upon his face. She is not afraid: she is in an ecstasy of love and admiration: she has found something to surpass her hopes. They remain for some seconds without moving.

Then a tall clock in the corner strikes two beats from its deep heart of oak.

CHAPTER V.

A GOLDEN HOUR

'Two o'clock.'

'Ah! we have not another hour; but I shall be able to drive you to the station; we can do it in twenty minutes.'

She rises without thanking him: details of time and distance—those are for him to decide.

Meanwhile they have very nearly an hour to spend together—how enjoy it best?

She walks away from the table and contemplates the room critically; as she does so she smiles at the history told by the little luncheon-table.

'*Ami* John, do you generally use all these plates and dishes?'

John shakes his head ruefully: deceptions

have never been in his line. He is at a
loss.

'*Enfin*, we must clear our own table, and
efface my record.'

This domestic concern makes their inter-
course easier. It seems to soften off the edge
of steepness from their conversation. Waldine's
plate and glass are washed by John's own
hands and set, by hers, in a particular corner
where his eye can rest upon them often. He
makes up the fire; she opens the window.
The beauty of the day is at its height still.

'Mild as May,' he says, as the soft air fans
him. He stands between the window and the
fireplace, and watches her throw out some
scraps of bread to the birds.

'See, John, there is a robin, and sparrows,
and a blackbird in the distance.'

'And presently the rooks will come, only
they see you. Do you hear the thrush?

> ' " 'Twas the thrush sang in the woodland—hear
>   the story, hear the story !—
> And the lark sang 'give us glory,' and the dove
>   sang 'give us peace.' " '

Surely John's dinner-room has never echoed any bird's song sweeter than her voice!

'Will you do me a favour?' he says in a tone that does not anticipate refusal.

'Yes.'

'Come into the next room and sing to me. There is my small piano there; you opened it but you did not play.'

'I was not at home with you then as I am now. Yes, we will sing something: what shall it be?'

He opens the door into the passage and she walks before him into the opposite room.

'When I come to live here I shall make this room so pretty,' she says laughing.

It is a new thought for John—another dream for his Arabian nights of enchantment.

'What will you do?' he asks her.

'I will have only the piano and a little wicker table and two wicker chairs, with some Turkish mats, upon those nice oak boards. And then plants and flowers—oh! endless flowers.'

'But where are the flowers to come from in December? we have no hot-houses here.'

'*Qu'importe?* Mr. Denham shall bring the flowers.'

John's face clouds : she feels that he is grave and turns quickly towards him.

'No!' he says, 'Mr. Denham shall not bring the flowers ; I will build you a conservatory and fill it with hyacinths, and we can have lilies and cyclamens too—our own flowers, not his.'

She listens to his voice which, whenever he speaks fervently, seems to mesmerise her into assent,—the spell of his manhood.

' Very well,' she says dreamily, and sits down to the piano.

She plays a *prélude* of Chopin—the sort of music his little Broadwood has never echoed before—and then she sings a setting of Vivien's song from the ' Idylls of the King '—

> ' In love, if love be love, if love be ours,
>   Faith and unfaith can ne'er be equal powers,
>   Unfaith in aught is want of faith in all.'

It is a very simple setting of the words, but John's heart approves it.   He is seated close to the piano, almost facing her as she sings. . . . He loves her ' all in all.'

'So you see that you must trust me altogether,' she says, when she has finished.

'It's done,' he answers her decisively:—'Do not think I have been pondering about it. Remember that it is *your* life which is complex, mine is single and plain.'

'"Single and plain," like an old maid,' she says, evading the recurrence of his serious mood. She leans forward on the keys with her face resting on her hands, and looking full into his eyes she laughs. 'John, is it not strange that our life here does not seem to me future but present—I had almost said past? I cannot think of it with apprehension. I suppose I ought to think gravely of its chances, with a resolve, in event of fate spoiling it, to be an old maid—if not "*plain*," "*single*." But I don't. I feel to be on level ground, to be able to look far back and far forward, and there are no changes and no surprises.'

'I think it is your nature,' says John quietly; 'you are like a bird; you will sing in a cage, if you are there, as well as in a grove. Sing something else in this cage.'

Her fingers wander over the keys for an instant : she picks out the *cavatina* of Raff, then she stops abruptly. 'How strange it is that you should be so fond of music !' she says.

'Because I have to work ?' he answers her ; 'oh ! it is not unusual now. There is some sort of musical instrument in almost every farm-house, and generally it is the men who play and sing more than their wives and daughters.'

'Which reminds me. Find something that we shall sing together.'

He stands up and turns over a pile of music on the piano ; as he does so he is very near her. The piano is low, and his right hand is almost before her ; she lays her fair face caressingly upon his arm. He looks down quickly. Something in her drooping attitude and shamefaced silence touches him to infinite tenderness. He restrains his first impulse lest it should alarm her. She is so at rest in her trust of him that a kiss would disturb her. But her beauty is eloquent in its stillness and seems to demand an answer.

'Waldine,' he says, 'may all God's angels guard you ; you are the joy of my life ! You have made me so glad to-day, that for any pain your love may ever bring me, I forgive you now.'

'Somehow that was what I wanted you to say,' she replies presently, raising her head. The tears stand again in her beautiful, burning eyes.

'Here are my songs,' says John gently, 'but we have not many minutes now, and your talk is sweeter than my singing.'

'But I want to hear your voice. Oh! here are Mendelssohn's duets, John; let us sing this one !'

They sing together :—

> 'Oh ! wert thou in the cauld blast
>   On yonder lea, on yonder lea,
>   My plaidie to the angry airt
>   I'd shelter thee. . . .'

It is wonderful how their voices blend, and how their mood befits the strain.

> 'The desert were a paradise
>   If thou wert there, if thou wert there. . . .'

they sing.

With something very like a sob she breaks off suddenly. Her whole being seems melted into song and love. His steadfast eyes that watch her as she plays, his pure, true voice that matches them, his bodily presence which she has come so far to seek—they are the light, the sound, the air of her magic world. She sighs heavily and then gets up from the piano, pushing her chair away backwards not to touch him. There are things she could not bear.

' I cannot sing,' she says ; ' go and get the horse, I think it is time to go.'

The want of tenderness in her words does not make them untender. A complimentary phrase of departure would reveal less feeling than this *brusque* command. By the same token he makes no answer: he only looks at his watch and then goes out of the room.

She is quite still for a few moments, standing by the window, as her wont is, with her hands clasped behind her. The first thought that rouses her is a momentary wonder whether her famous ash-tree is visible from this house ;

but the wonder is too transitory for her to care to satisfy it by observation. It just acts in her brain the sort of part a dream is said to act in sleep—it serves for gradual awakening. Then she passes her hand over her eyes and looks back into the room.

'To think that he can live here!' she says beneath her breath.

Going away, he has taken more than he knew. He has, as it were, exposed the commonness of his poor little drawing-room: she sees it as it is. Sometimes a flood of sunshine will make an ordinary object beautiful: the sun goes in, and its ugliness appals one. Now that the sunshine of her heart is gone, this empty place of it looks hideous and barren. In a sort of reaction from her trivial surroundings, she glances down on a beautiful gold pencil that hangs by her side; her fingers adjust it and its use occurs to her. There is a blotting-book on the table in front of her; she takes a scrap of paper from between its leaves, and placing it against the window-pane she writes these words :—

' *When you play music, close your eyes and think of me. My home is in your heart.*'

With an impulse to give something to him in remembrance of this golden hour, she unfastens the pencil-case and rolls it up in the scrap of paper. Her desire is to leave some trace behind her which shall be more beautiful than the details of her lover's daily life ; the impulse is not entirely unselfish. She walks back to the piano and lays the little packet on the keys, closing the case. With that curious trust in circumstances which with her is half instinct and half carelessness, she is sure that his hands will be the first to find it. Then she quietly returns to the less decorated room which pleases her so much better, and puts on her hat and jacket without going to the glass.

She has done with the scene of this episode. That is her feeling. Thoroughly sincere as she is in her love, she is without that intimate affection for place and objects which character- ises her sex. The passion that has possessed her is too concentrated, too large, to let her trouble much about its accidents. This particular act of life's drama is over : the stage on which it has been played is nothing to her but a platform that has served its turn. As she slowly draws on her tan gloves she does not even look about her. She has no wish for a mental photograph of the house where her seat is set.

Meanwhile John is mindful of her departure. A few minutes have sufficed him to harness the Denham mare and brush the cushions of his little country cart. He makes all haste, for he too must find her some token of his devotion from among his few and simple worldly goods.

When he comes downstairs from ransacking his treasures he meets her in the hall.

'Will you take this?' he says, 'the words are in what always seems to me your native language.'

He has a quaint old oval case in his hand, glass, with a gold rim. Long years ago it was a gift to some forefather of his from the woman to whose tragic fate he has made allusion—the woman from whom he has inherited his peculiar beauty. It contains a tress of dark hair, on which rests a delicate ivory tablet shaped into a heart; on the tablet, in fine black letters, like old-fashioned penmanship, are the words, ' *Ton amitié fait mon joie;*' round it and above it a thread of gold is twined into a true-lover's knot. Intrinsically of no great value, it is the kind of token which a sympathetic mind regards with reverence. It has been the sign, it is still the memorial, of the heart's desire. To some one, at some time, it has seemed worth the world beside.

She takes the present in her hand and reads the posy in her clear foreign accents. ' It is written wrong,' she says, ' but it is very pretty. *Ami* John, there is something I want, of which this reminds me. I want a bit of your hair. Do you think we could undo this to hold it : the rim is slight ?'

He holds the locket, looking at it critically ; it had never occurred to him that she would want to tamper with it, but he does not

gainsay her wish. He takes his knife from
his pocket and begins to unfasten the soldered
edges. In a moment they give way; the
fragile token has held its treasure for an
hundred years, but it yields to the first rough
touch of this utilitarian day.

'Bring it in here,' she says, going back into
the room; 'we have only a moment.'

Glass, rims, tablet, hair, gold thread—the
whole contents of the little gift, which seems
to have lost its charm in the undoing—lie on
the table before them.

'Kneel down,' says the girl laughing, 'and
give me that knife. Ah! John, it is the
knife I stabbed you with.'

She lets it drop quickly, and, falling, it
breaks one of the thin convex glasses of the
locket.

'It is broken I fear,' says John in amazed
sorrow, picking up the pieces as he stoops; it
seems to him, somehow, to be an irretrievable
loss, as indeed it is, to Time.

'Ah! what a pity! But never mind. I
do not greatly care for ornaments. Mr.

Denham said just the other evening that it was odd, when I told him I only liked diamonds.'

' 'And I shall never have any diamonds to give you.'

'You! oh! the gift you give me—that is different. No, John, no: I do not want that relic, put it all into your pocket together. Are these your mother's scissors?'

He kneels down before her with his dark head bent. She has ungloved her hands again, and she passes them lightly over his curly hair till she severs a thick lock of it which twines round her fingers. She puts it down on the table with the scissors and then bends over her lover and hesitates for a moment.

' *Tu es bien à moi,*' she says, rapidly as a breath, and her lips touch his hair like flame. It is not a kiss. He could not say whether it was her cheek or her hand that touched him. He reads the passion of her tone into a kind of benediction, for he has not caught her words. But he puts his arms round her as he kneels, and his head leans against her waist.

The warmth and peculiar softness of the seal-skin coat she wears almost overpower his senses: the moment feels eternal: when he stirs he could fancy himself awaking from a long sleep or a swoon, and his eyes are heavy and hot.

As for her, she will lose it never, that feeling of support and possession which his clasping arms and throbbing forehead press beneath her beating, yielding heart. There springs to life in her the maternal element of loving: she pities him for his pain in losing her; as she frees herself there is compassion in her hands and her voice is sad.

'Come,' she says kindly, as if she would console him, 'I shall lose my train.'

He pockets the *débris* of the broken trinket, saving only the gold thread which he twists round the lock of hair before she places it within her glove in the hollow of her hand.

'It is a clumsy keepsake,' he says shyly; 'you ought to have cut it better.'

'Yes, I have spoilt your head: I hope you are not like Samson: I should be sorry to steal your strength.'

'And am I to have nothing?' He glances at her wind-ruffled hair with wistful eyes.

'There is no time: I do not want *my* head spoilt: that matters. I will send you a yard of hair if you like; but it means nothing to me to give it you. I am not sentimental, John, and you must not be. Why I wanted this, was for a sign of your existence: I am not going to cherish it that I know of. It is a proof to me that you exist and that, existing, you are mine.'

'Never doubt that,' he answers with a sigh: he does not question her will: his heart has no such need of tokens, but his sigh reproves her: she glances off the subject.

'If you want a sign of my existence,' she says laughing, 'look in the glass, if the wound in your wrist is healed. For I have not only stabbed you, but I have taken your scalp. John, I feel that I have behaved like a wild Indian.'

'Like Longfellow's Minnehaha?' says John with a smile,—'the laughing water.'

They are standing upright now, facing each

other, and it seems to each of them that the other's presence is all the world contains. The mutual photograph upon their brains must be a clear one, focused by such ardent eyes. The afternoon is so quiet that they hear the Denham mare pawing the flagstones of the yard where John has tied her. She is not used to waiting before she begins her journeys.

She warns them of the flight of time : their thoughts are in such unison that they do not need exchange the warning. John reaches down his hat and they go out.

It is already colder, and he does not stay for a coat : is not the beating of his heart enough to warm him to his feet and finger tips? He has never taken any woman but his mother in this little cart of his, which is a new purchase of Lord Grenvers'. He has had no experience in life like this drive with Waldine down his favourite lanes, where there is not a single passer-by to look at them askance. The sense of doubled life, the satisfaction of the company of this beloved and lovely woman,—it makes all fresh as paradise was fresh to Adam after the birth of Eve.

And Waldine's contentment is absolute ; the swift motion, for their time is short, the light noise of the wheels, the fanning air—above all, the sense of moving towards a goal, which is ever a joy to her—make all her senses keen in the crystal day. Seated at his side, warm in her close fine fur, she takes long looks up to his face when his eyes are occupied with the mare. She feels to know that face so well, to love it so dearly. And is it not the most beautiful thing in the world ? Her heart brims over with possession and pride. The way the cool air darkens and pales his cheek, the rare closing of his lips to a soft encouraging whistle which the Denham mare quite understands without a touch from the whip—these things, which are lessons to her, do not seem strange : it vaguely occurs to her that when she drives in London she will miss them.

Nor is he silent now : the familiar scenes through which they pass are potent instigants to speech. He tells her all his days: he explains to her the country-side.   She knows the road, but she has driven it hitherto alone or talking *chiffons* with Lady Grenvers : it has been a sealed record to her till now, of which he can unfold the story.   They only stop for one instant just to catch full view of Whiteknyghts with its great array of shining windows.

'Yes, I see it,' says the girl smiling—'big, empty shrine of the "dear saint."—Ah ! *mon ami*, if I were not here would you be there ? '

'Of course,' says John, smiling too.   He is so happy that he can afford to make light of his own constancy.

'I wonder what her ladyship would say if she met us.   But, John, do you know, she never sees any one : she always says to me, "Here is a carriage, Val, how am I looking ? " and when the carriage has passed, she says, "Who was it ?   How did I look ? " '

'Then she may meet us and welcome,' says John : he hums a little air and then adds, breaking it off short, 'Is that what she calls you ? '

'That is what I am mostly called ; "Waldine"

is strange and formal : no one has ever called
me that.'

'May I?' says John : it is the first direct
request he has made her. 'The "lady of the
woodlands?" I should like to call you that.'

'Very well,' she says contentedly, 'I am
Waldine to you. Val to the rest of the world.'

'And Miss de Stair to Mr. Denham?'

'If you will : but you call your horse the
Denham mare.'

'Will you christen her another name?'

'You can call her Countess Val.'

He looks troubled. 'I always forget your
foreign dignity,' he says : 'does it matter?'

'Nothing matters,' she answers, looking up
anxiously at his face, 'except——'

His eyes meet hers : it is a long straight
road : the Denham mare has settled down into
a steady trot which she will not break till they
near the station hill where John and his love
must part. He gathers the reins into his
right hand and puts his left arm, being human,
round her waist.

'Oh! that is safe,' he says in a low tone,

and then he draws her towards him and his lips stoop to hers. Lovers of old time, long dead, does not your dust thrill at their meeting? . . . Was the road so short? was the pace so fleet? they have reached the station turning, and a shrill whistle sounds on the bright air, almost in their ears.

'Just in time!' says the girl, panting with fresh haste as she descends:—'No, John; another yard and they will see you: I can run these few steps more—Good-bye!'

He leans over the cart, but she is on foot already and she does not once look back. Where is the good of looking at him when her eyes are drowned with tears—most sudden tears— of bliss? Where is the good of looking at him when his seal is set upon her mouth and his image on her heart for ever?

John Lyne drives down to Netherfield in the afternoon, as it changes to chill. He goes a long way round, he will not return to his empty house. His face grows cold, his hands numb, but his brain is dizzy and his pulses throb. He has entered into the world of unrest: he will know no more careless days and no more dreamless nights. His life is set henceforward to the tune of this girl's voice. She has taken from him his strength and his peace ; she has left him nothing but the sweetness of her roseleaf lips on his.

She speeds through the gathering dusk, sitting alone and motionless in the railway carriage, feeling neither noise nor cold—spellbound, silent, warm. All goes so well with her. When she meets the carriage Mrs. Lupton's train is still not due ; when she meets Mrs. Lupton that lady is cross and tired, and insists on bringing Mr. Collington home to dine. His hotel is in Half Moon Street, and he can go on there in the brougham to dress while she slips on her tea-gown : they will have such a cosy evening !

'Dear Val, I'm afraid your time has been dull, but I hope you had a pleasant luncheon. You must tell me all about your day when you've heard mine. See, Cecil, what a hostess I am ! I ask her no questions, and then perhaps she won't ask *us* any. . . .' Mrs. Lupton's tone becomes suddenly lowered to the flirtation register. When they arrive in Curzon Street she has fifty notes to read ; there is also a letter for Waldine with the Whiteknyghts postmark, from her devoted aunt. It is too long to read at once, but the postscript attracts her eyes :—

'Poor John Lyne has been quite horridly ill—pleurisy or something : he is all right again, as far as he ever will be, but has lost his looks—*such a pity*, for you know I had the most idiotic *penchant* for his handsome face : no one could sympathise with it *now*, least of all you who hate invalids. Oh ! how he would bore you ! health was his charm. But who can be well in this arctic month ? I am *alive*, but see nobody : my nose is like a *damson :* is chinchilla *really* so much worn ? ask Charlotte. . . .'

'They are stupid and false,' says the girl to herself passionately, 'they shall never know.'

And she locks up that day in her soul and gives the key to memory.

CHAPTER VI.

WALDINE WRITES

CURZON STREET, *Christmas Eve.*

MY OWN DEAR LOVE!—These many days you have lain silent in my heart: I have had no need of speech. To-night you wake and call me: I rise and answer.

Why to-night? I do not know. I tell you always I am not sentimental: I do not believe that anything is happening to you that should distress me on your account. I do not think that you are ill or that you want me. But there are times and times in love. It has its moods like the sea —poor old *simile* that has done duty so often!—and to-night there is a full moon tide of speech. . . . I take you out of my deep heart and I look at you : I love you : let us take counsel together.

Confession first: *mon amour*, I have told nothing to anyone : I think you thought I should, but it was impossible. Life is intricate: to throw truth to people who don't know what truth is, you might as well feed a serpent on flowers! They cry out for something palpitating to mangle, these cobras of gossip ; and you and I will not be food for them. Do not look solemn about it. Trust me, and all will be well.

All *is* well. John, I wonder whether English girls often do what I have done—take an independent journey to satisfy their . . . caprice—curiosity—what was it? and then return to find that they have not been missed and nothing is said. I feel I did a dreadful thing, but it is not because I am found out; rather, I think, because I am so scot-free, and my world rolls along so evenly again after the kick I gave it. I have proved Mrs. Lupton's maxim true : 'The big things of life remain unknown.' But for all that they are not unimportant.

What are you doing? I do not ask: I know. You are asleep and you dream of me. It is what I am doing that I want to tell you, obedient to one of your last suggestions. You were right to make it: it is good for me to unfold myself to you. You are the peace and the calm of my days: I feel myself nervous and modern in face of your old-time simplicity and strength. All about you and around you now there is the immense quiet of the winter night: leagues upon leagues of unbroken silence which the town noises never reach.

John, I think of you in your little house as it were in a safe grave. It seems to me possible —happily possible—to turn my back upon the town, to go far and to dig deep and to find—you: and this 'return upon you' is the mainspring of my life. Here is my tendril token of your hair before me on the table. I think out all the way to you—the loud and crowded terminus here, the long journey into ever purer air, the small country station, the hill, the road we went together, the lane to your garden-gate, the pathway with the roses at the end. I pass up that pathway: I stand at the barred door. I do not knock, I enter. It is all so still that I can think I hear the snow fall. There is no light in the passage now, no light in either room I know, but I do not stumble: I go ghostlike up the stair. Yes, you are safe at home, but you are not safe from me. I come to you with the burden of my life, with all its desires and sighs. And at your door I knock. Oh! my love, do you sleep still? Do you not hear my tears upon your threshold? must they fall there? . . .

Was it a thunderbolt? was it a storm that scared the vision? Nothing, John, nothing but the rumbling of some market-cart that goes belated or beforehand up the street. Here market-carts, and worse than market-carts, are for ever scaring my visions. I feel as if I had got into the heart of some great beating machine, for which the fuel is the lives of men. Sometimes when I look out of my window I thank God for frost or rain. At least they are signs to me that there *are* elements somewhere which bring gifts of whiteness and wet. My window at White-knyghts—I pant for it, I cannot stay longer away. Every day it has some new surprise for me ; some sober glory of winter colour, some group of sheep or cattle that are at home there and at ease. There is a farmer pastures his cows in the park ; at eight in the morning I see them bounding over the grass. There is a gladness in the rustle of their paces, crisp on the snow or thudding in the thaw. It makes me happy to hear the beasts begin their free and open day. A whole long day, it must be so much to a cow or a sheep ! Here too it may be much, but it is a muchness of the wrong order—like a day in the shambles for them.

John, 'my *whole* day,' was I to tell it you ? Then it shall be to-day : that's easy. You don't know what a London fog is ; I shall not attempt to describe it. One feels as if one were sitting under the shadow of some awful and mysterious sorrow. One can imagine one's self in hell. Sisyphus, Ixion, Tantalus—

in turn one is each and all.   Mrs. Lupton has
a special *régime* for fogs when she is in the
mood to avoid them.   For there are days
when she is *in the vein:* then she goes out,
and heaven knows what befalls her!   To-day,
however, she was not willingly befogged, and
she fought the stars in their courses.   Every
shutter was shut, every blind was down; we
played at its being evening.   All the pretty
lamps were lit in the *boudoir;* they would
amuse you, some of them, supported by
flamingoes, owls and peacocks—quite literally
'ivory and apes and peacocks;'—we wore
dressing-gowns and discussed our neighbours.
What we did? we chose evening frocks,
availing ourselves of the various lights; mine
is yellow—an appalling colour by daylight,
like the yolk of an egg.   Faithful to her
appointment, a dressmaker appeared about
them, and things of so much moment are
not decided in an hour.   Mr. Collington came
to luncheon of course and brought a couple of
young actors with him, who delighted in the
artificial glow and the real banquet.   They

are getting up a little comedy with Mrs.
Lupton as the heroine, and they rehearsed it
in the afternoon : I stayed in the drawing-
room while they went to the empty music-
room, and before answering some notes I took
up a novel. The fog and the lamps together
had given me a headache, and I went to sleep
—which is perhaps the reason why I cannot
sleep to-night, dear comrade of my vigil, and
perhaps it is not why ! I went to sleep and I
dreamed.—Of you ? Yes, first, and then that
Mr. Denham called—and behold ! it was not
a dream ! I awoke and rubbed my eyes ; he
was there in the flesh. What he said ? John,
you are tedious in your demands : I don't
remember. *Yes I do.* He gave me various
most interesting personal statistics, to which
I listened while I sat and wished that he were
you. He told me who his tailor was and
where he got his flowers ; and that he liked
the roses *on* my tea-gown, and that he liked
the set *of* my tea-gown, and that he liked me
in my tea-gown. Which was no trouble and
the reverse of unpleasant, but which did not,

if you will believe it, amuse me in the least.

And then I told him what I thought of him : I said I thought he was part of the 'fuel' for the machine of life in town and in the country, to which he replied that he was very *inflammable;* and what with the sleep and the dream I felt so far away from him all the while that I said, 'Really, do you know, that's not at all bad for you,' without in the least remembering that I was speaking to a real man. At which he was good enough to laugh not unkindly :—he is not unkind.

John, I am glad you are not rich and do not wear button-hole bouquets. Mrs. Lupton said the other day that she 'never got any tonic out of a scent-bottle.' I am much of her mind. It keeps one awake, it refreshes even, but that is the most one can say to praise it.

Perhaps, however, Mr. Denham is more than a scent-bottle ; for—I had half forgotten it—he became rather serious before our *tête-à-tête* was interrupted. He referred again to the

demise of his mamma—which made me laugh,
the dear defunct being obviously resuscitated
only as the keystone to more vital relationship.
I suggested that Mrs. Lupton would be a
mother to him gladly if he would allow her.

'And you a sister, do you mean?' he said
imploringly.

I did not quite see how that followed, but
I admitted that the limit of my years would
allow of the relationship. And even then he
was not satisfied; he said he did not want a
sister. 'Then,' I concluded brilliantly, 'I
shall have to be a mother to you myself.'
And upon that imaginative basis our friendship
rests for the present.—What! my real love,
you are not laughing? you look puzzled but
not amused? I hear you say, in that grave
voice of yours, that you do not want to be
Mr. Denham's stepfather. Very well, then,
very well: all that you wish is very well
to me. Yes! best of all.

That's now; and which of us two, dear,
shall mind about the future? That tiresome
future, it is buried deep enough this winter

while; we shall not hear it start till spring. Are you not satisfied? Then come and see for yourself. London is not so far.

I went to you once—did I not, or is it all a dream?—I cannot come again. Mrs. Lupton's expeditions are ended for this winter; she took cold on that last journey, and is always saying how fortunate I was to have been safe at home. My conscience does not sting me, for if ever I was 'safe at home' it was then; with you, John, with you.

Persistent still? I have said, 'Come and see! come and see that I do not forget you!' but you want to know these little things, and somehow, all the time, I want to tell you them. Mr. Denham informs me that the filial relationship demands a certain confidence; I reply that my time and my attention are at his disposal on foggy days. He remarks that he hopes it will be foggy all the winter; I rejoin that I have every fear his wish may be fulfilled. There is then a long pause. Am I sufficiently dramatic? for you know the accents of the dialogue. After the pause he said that

he congratulated — was it himself or me?
—that he had got so far. It seemed to me
that he had 'got' not forward but backward
many weary years, as I found myself with so
full-grown a son, and I ventured that witticism
as well. To which he replied that anything
which neared us to each other seemed a step
forward to him. And, while I thought just
that same thought of *you*, you may guess that
I was not slow to retort to *him* that I found he
was 'quite forward enough' already!

And it was almost directly after that repartee that Mrs. Lupton came into the room,
triumphant from the completed rehearsal. . . .
As for us two, John, we are near enough!

How cold it is! with fire and gas and
lamps I do not feel it here, but I know how
keen the frost is by all the little signs of
London winter—the way the flames burn, the
sounds one hears far off, the sleep, like a thick
cloak, that is upon one the instant one seeks
it. And you sleep sound, I know, nearer
Nature than I, in the home that will be mine
one day.

Oh! love, love! there is no rose left in your garden pathway now! but this room is full of roses . . . and they are not all artificial roses either, for my adopted son sent me a bouquet this evening in which there are real rosebuds almost sweet. We went to the first night of a new burlesque; when I returned I found *you* waiting in my room and sent away my maid. . . . Here you still are, but I have failed to write you my day, failed in the expression of all I would express, only will not fail in the expression of my love! I love you more than you love me, more than you know that I can love. You think of other things than love, you think *I* think of other things than those; I think of one thing only, love, I think of you! No future planned; believe I want no future—that will come. No past remembered, for I have no memory of the past—*it* was not yours!—But *I* am yours,

WALDINE.

Come to me! when you will, as you will, only somehow come! I want to prove you mine.

CHAPTER VII.

FROST

PROOF? what proof was needed? Was he not hers as wholly as the thorn-stem is the grafted rose's? He had no separate existence now, no aim in life but just to be the standard of her pride. How best to serve her? He received the letter on the 26th of December; the letter said, 'Come,' and he went next morning.

It was difficult, but there is a providence for lovers: Lord Grenvers had long been wanting a locomotive couch, adapted specially to his infirmities; it had been an old suggestion of his that John Lyne should pay his first visit to London-town in quest of this, and at the same time he could take an ornament to

Curzon Street, which was Lady Grenvers' Christmas gift to Val, and which thus need not risk the laden post. It was all settled in five minutes, and settled without sacrifice of truth.

Lady Grenvers had said to John, 'It is *polar*; if I drive to Netherfield I die : you must order me some New Year cards; only there is no choice as there is in London.'

'I suppose the London shops are very gay just now,' he said in tentative reply.

'What a wistful voice!' put in his lordship, whose daily interview with John Lady Grenvers had unceremoniously interrupted, 'I believe you'd like to go and see them!'

'I *should* like to go to London,' said John frankly,' with a sort of passive wonder.

'And you shall,' cried her ladyship; 'and take Val her pendant: I shall never wear that pearl pendant again, Grenvers; it was one of your first presents to me and is only fit for a girl! And Val has so few things. It will still be in the family, and he can get your *chaise longue*—order it, at least—and bring

me my New Year cards. Could you not go
to-morrow ? I really want them.'

'Yes, gladly,' said John, who felt his heart
bound at the possibilities afloat towards him
on the spell of the easy placid voice. And
gladly, when to-morrow came, he went. Another time it would have seemed a great event
this going to London ; it seemed less than
nothing now, as a mile walk is apt to seem a
step in the direction of the beloved. There
were subjects to be considered ; but not in
relation to London, only in relation to one
feminine atom befogged therein whose eyes
were poor John's lodestars. There was the
question of dress, there was the question of
times, there was the question of behaviour.
To look worthy of her, to reach her and to be
what she would have him be—this was the
triple problem which extinguished all wonder
as it annulled all distance.

Before Lady Grenvers sent the pearl pendant
across the park to John's home it had flashed
above her mental horizon that she might be
promoting a possible meeting between her

niece and him. But it only occurred to her
as the light for another lamp of self-approba-
tion. She wrote outside the packet, 'To be
left at 90 Curzon Street, Mrs. Lupton's ; *you
need not ask for Mrs. Lupton,*' and slept
soundly under the warm glow of her discretion.
He will have plenty else to do, she thought.

So John registered a mental vow that he
would not ' ask for Mrs. Lupton,' and snatched
his few hours' sleep with a conscience only at
all disturbed by the triple problem. And
when he woke ere daybreak it was solved.
He would just let things slide ; no forethought
thus far could have bettered fate's. He dressed
himself at dawn in his plain Sunday clothes ;
that they were not the clothes in vogue never
suggested itself to him, nor did he balance in
his mind whether they became him as well as
the costume of his daily wear. They were his
better clothes ; there was no choice. In his
breast-pocket was the box containing the
pendant, laid alongside of Waldine's letters,
and therefore safe with his life ; in an outer
pocket was a card on which his name was

written and his address, in case mishap befell him. London was for him a sort of violent engine, like the train. 'If I'm killed anywhere, they shan't have to find her letter to know my home.'

What he looked like? Very like a gentleman, only a touch more manly than most. The boots were not very shapely and the hat was wrong, but the walk was such as a prince might have envied, and the head was as handsome as a god's. His covert coat was permissible in town as in the fields ; its earthy tint became him very well : the general effect was sombre.

'Why, John,' said Mrs. Lyne, 'where's your coloured scarf? you don't look half smart for London.'

'Oh! I'm not going a holiday, mother,' he answered :—' It's sober earnest this is, and lots to think of.'

And much he did think in the train and much in the streets, but it was not much of London. It was one thought only—' Waldine, Waldine, I come!'

After his four hours' journey, for the morning train was slow, the day seemed younger in the city streets than he had left it at Netherfield. He had this day before him, for there was a late train back; and he found himself in the neighbourhood of the shops for his commissions.

It did not strike John to drive: he walked gravely along the foggy thoroughfares; visited the place, somewhere in the Strand, for Lord Grenvers' couch; and made his way through Soho into Regent Street for her ladyship's cards. There was an embarrassing choice. He looked in window after window till perplexity as well as dust was on his face.

'Perhaps,' he said to himself at last, 'perhaps *she* would. . . .'

It was half-past one o'clock; he did not feel hungry. He went down Conduit Street and Bruton Street. Berkeley Square! they had told him that was near his goal.

Afterwards John remembered best of all his London wanderings the last time he asked his way to 90 Curzon Street. It was just opposite to Lansdowne House, where the statue stood dripping under leafless boughs in shivering feminine contrast to a well-clad policeman who was contemplating her with unsympathetic contempt. Mrs. Lupton would have delighted in the contrast between his stalwart warmth and that modest chill of hers which was so much more permanent. And the group detached that lady's image in John's mind.

'Does Mrs. Lupton live about here?' asked John.

'I beg your pardon, sir,' said the astonished policeman; and then after a second glance, which somehow flushed John's temples, he added, 'I suppose you're from the country; don't you know the address?'

It was rather a blow to John Lyne, and he was glad that the subsequent direction should be plain even to a rustic intelligence, unaware that of two easy routes his informant chose the less direct—'Back a bit and down Berkeley Street; past the bottom of 'Ay 'Ill; then down the little tunnel to the right, and there you are.'

It was very foggy, very cold, very still. He skirted the dead wall and there was the old-fashioned passage, looking like a vault with its iron pillar and grimy steps.

' Well,' said John to himself, ' it's not as fine as the lodge at Whiteknyghts.'

He swung himself down the stairs : the clank of his footsteps, echoing along the narrow walls, amused him : perhaps it was his quickened walking that made this sudden heat and glow about him ; his whole frame tingled as he went. Perhaps. . . .

He stopped quite still ; he could not have advanced a step.

' Waldine !'

She had entered the passage from the Curzon Street end : indeed it was none other than she, and, by a final miracle, she was alone. Surely nothing could befall her between Curzon Street and Dover Street, where she was going to luncheon with some friends arrived from abroad. Nothing did befall her, but just this : to find the radiant moment of her life upon the muddy way. So one finds Love.

She was looking exquisitely lovely ; even her beauty could be heightened by contrast with dark fur and the rich velvets of Mrs. Lupton's choice. She had dressed herself with unusual care, and in this dingy frame and under this gray sky she was the very picture of luxury and grace. She walked lightly and demurely ; her femininity divined a man whom she must pass—her air was the more reserved —her eyelids proudly drooped.

She came quite close to him : he spoke aloud, ' Waldine.'

Pace from motion to stillness : lips from red to white : heart from life to death. And then with one soft word, with one short step, back to red lips and fuller life again.

No one came by : the world was going to luncheon, and the world's underlings had ceased purveying it. It was the *siesta* of the little dark passage and this word its midday dream. . . .

' You see I have come,' he said at last, smoothing her hair with his hand where his lips had stirred it, for she seemed as if she could not speak to him; 'and it wasn't so difficult either; there were things to be done, and luckily it fell to me to do them. . . .'

'Never mind,' she answered, her senses returning with the tints of her cheek, 'you are here and we have met; you were coming to find me.'

'I was coming to leave a case of trinkets for you, from Lady Grenvers; I was specially told not to ask for Mrs. Lupton.'

'And you would not have asked for her; would you have asked for me?'

'I don't know; it seemed all bound to come right somehow. Will you have the trinkets?'

'No:—what do they matter? you can leave them by and by. John! are you glad to see me?'

'Very glad; but must you be always as finely dressed as this in London?'

She sighed. 'No, I suppose not; but I like clothes, and I am going to such a luncheon party—the De Loëwes',—oh! you don't know —and to meet royalty.'

'Princes and princesses?'

'Not the whole Almanach De Gotha, John—
one English princess and some foreign poten-
tates. I knew the De Loëwes well in Brussels;
they are at Brown's hotel. The worst of
royalty is that one can't be late, and I don't
see my way to being ill at a moment's notice.'

'No,' said John directly, 'you must go.
What time will it be over?'

'I can get away at three. Meet me here
then. What shall you do meanwhile?'

'Leave the parcel at Mrs. Lupton's.'

'It will take five minutes, and there is an
hour and a half before you. Perhaps I can
escape before three, but Mrs. Lupton thinks I
shall stay the whole afternoon.'

'I will wait for you here; come when you
can. But Waldine, answer me one question.
Do you care for all this—I mean this gaiety
and pleasure? You are so young, you are so
bright and rare.'

'You speak of me as if I were a gem, only
then youth would not add to my value. John,
yes, I care for it all: don't let me undervalue
or underrate things. I care for clothes and

compliments.   But I care more for you; even
with that same *me* which these things occupy
I care more for you than for them.   You are
the great excitement of my life, the thing that
is most at my heart is to tell you how entirely
I love you.'

'Oh, Waldine, Waldine, do you speak the
truth?'

'Absolutely.   Walk demurely now, as you
saw me walking : there is some one coming
and I feel I am not behaving well.   *Why in
heaven's name haven't you got a high hat on?*'

'Is it wrong—this hat?   I never thought
—and my coat?'

Looking down from the hat to the coat,
she had to meet the eyes, so that the coat was
never commented upon : she laughed lightly
under her breath and they let the stranger
pass them.

'What shall we do this afternoon?   Have
you any sort of plan?'

'I am to get some New Year cards for
Lady Grenvers.'

'The very thing : we will go to a shop I

know of together, and choose them; I shall buy a thick veil, and then we can go in a hansom. It is very shocking, but it does not strike me as wrong. Does it you?'

'Don't do it another day with Mr. Denham.'

'Not with my son? John, what a look! He will be at the luncheon: I wish I could take you. But you would hate it and I should hate you there; if you looked at the princess I should die of jealousy. Do get a high hat, there are plenty of shops in Bond Street. It will be something for you to do, and I am sure it will suit you. What is the time?'

'Ten minutes to two.'

'I must go.'—They were standing on the steps near the pillar.—'Wish me a pleasant morning! I shall be thinking of you all the while.'

'Think of me thus!'

He had taken her softly in his arms before she was aware; 'Waldine!' he said, 'my wife.'

It was a whisper, like a breath of June. Ah! how he loved her: even her exactions were contented now.—That tenderness of his embrace, that lover's utter gift of self—they must have left a gust of summer between the dark walls, a shock of warmth in the cold pillar, for the next fortunate passer-by. What was it wandering in the air? a soul exchanged —or lost?

'*A bientôt*,' she said; and then, for there were footsteps, she was gone.

He watched her cross the road and walk with supple easy motion up Hay Hill. Then he went through the passage again without seeing a yard of it: and luckily he could not miss his way to Mrs. Lupton's house.

He had an hour before him: he went to Bond Street and bought himself a hat.

'I want a high hat, please,' he said, 'like they are wearing now.'

It was the latest defect licensed: it made him look very tall, and it was not quite easy on his curly head. Moreover, it cost a great deal of money; that mattered more.

In effect he had left himself a margin of thirty shillings for the day's expenses, of which the hat took twenty-five. But five shillings

would suffice for his refreshment, and he had
not told his mother that he had thought of
bringing her a present from London. He put
on the new hat and pocketed the change: he
gave up that notion of a present for his
mother.

'Where shall I send your other hat, sir?'

He did not think of having it sent to the
station: he did not want to give an address:
'Will you keep it for me till I call?' he said.

(So that perhaps John's hat is at the hatters
still!)

He had a travelling cap in his pocket, that
would do for the train. As for the new one,
he would slink in, at home, and hide it, or
throw it out of the carriage window before he
reached Netherfield: he knew it was an useless
purchase, but it was Waldine's wish that he
should have it—it seemed like the price of his
blissful hour with her.

'Now for some dinner,' he said, as he left
the shop. He had a sovereign that Lady
Grenvers had sent him for the New Year
cards; he must keep that intact: he had his

return ticket and he had five shillings : he was hungry and would have no further expenses.

Stay ! the cab in which he was to drive with Waldine by and by ?

He stood still outside the Grosvenor restaurant and whistled softly.

Then he took his hand out of his pocket and buttoned his coat.

He had breakfasted betimes and it was long past his dinner-hour, but there was no help for it, he could not afford to dine now. If he could get some bread and cheese ?

But that is a difficulty in Bond Street. There was a baker's : but by some odd chain of influences his high hat prevented his going there. He had a feeling that it would look unusual. On the whole, it was easier to be hungry. 'By Jove,' he said, 'I would eat my hat if I could.' He could hardly return, however, to the shop that he had honoured with his patronage and offer there the old hat in exchange for a meal. He had put on an instinct with his London chimney-pot and he was obliged to obey it. Neither bright

public-house, discharging muddy workmen,
nor pastry-cooks, with supercilious Hebe,
satisfied the requirements of this instinct.
He took exercise instead of luncheon. It was
not so strengthening, but it was cheaper.

The shops bewildered him with their show
of jewels and silks; but one would not have
guessed his wonderment. Like all country-
bred Englishmen, he had a shyness which
looked very like pride. It was the first time
that this shyness had absolutely gnawed his
vitals, but in the extreme form it shaped
itself into extreme reserve; just because he
was hungry and shy, his air was consequential
in its nobleness and languor.

People looked at him too; perhaps what
was attractive in his aspect was that it was
not yet levelled to the ordinary London tone.
Without being odd he had the impropriety of
being brilliantly handsome, and of having the
flesh-tints not effaced by lassitude or dirt.
The hour passed very quickly; his mind
photographed all sorts of pictures—carriages,
horses, corners, faces, but he was unaware of

most of them; it was an automatic process. It was only when he turned into Grafton Street again and saw the Bond Street panorama still before his eyes that he knew he had observed intently, that he knew he should remember. He was in Berkeley Street at ten minutes to three: she might escape, she had said, before the appointed hour. He waited a quarter of an hour, half an hour, an hour—patient as a dog. It rained. He sheltered himself under the portico of the passage and made skirmishes of observation. Presently from his covert he saw Waldine in a hansom with Mr. Denham: she fronted John as they drove down Hay Hill: she was laughing—he could see that; her lips were like a scarlet flower, her teeth like millet; but he could not see the way her eyes sought out his figure in the dark. Despite his hunger and chill, he felt a great access of angry jealousy inflame him. He would not be the first to drive with her that day then, despite her having characterised the proceeding as very shocking?

He had told her rightly what his simple

country-breeding meant, with its heritage of single-hearted passion. He could renounce her; he had hardly sought the boon she had bestowed on him; but he could not share her with another. She would have to understand that, once and for all.

He straitened himself up almost fiercely and lit a cigar to calm his nerves; the look in his eyes as the match showed them was a look of heavy care. How long he might have to wait he did not know, but it never occurred to him to go elsewhere. Her word was law.

A sudden rattle of wheels round the corner of the square—her radiant face was before him again; she was alone in the hansom now; that flamelike vision burnt up all the smoke of jealousy and wrath.

'Stop,' she called out to the driver, 'stop! there's my—brother! . . .'

And then she fell back laughing and covered her burning face with her hands.

'Oh John,' she said, 'how different you look to Launcelot in London!'

CHAPTER VIII.

FIRE

JOHN got into the hansom dexterously enough, considering the difficulties of the vehicle, only bruising the unaccustomed hat against the drooping glass. As he settled himself beside her it seemed to him that Waldine expanded like some lovely tropical flower; the sweetness of her presence made his heart faint with longing. Excitement, flattery and delicate fare had all been to her a sort of prelude to this feast of love. She was warm in every limb; her sapphire eyes and vivid lips flashed smiles; and this meeting long deferred was to be the crown of her delight.

That John was jealous, hungry, cold—ill with the weary and unusual day—never once

occurred to her mind. Was anger possible?
were there such terrors as fatigue and chill?
How should she know? she felt like a fairy
queen, commissioned to fling glory through
the town with her fairy prince beside her.

'Shut the doors,' she said, still laughing, ' I
have told him where to go! What I have
been through to come to you! your providence almost failed us. . . . I was in such a
hurry to get away that they all wanted to
know my plans. Mr. Denham said he should
walk back with me; then I said I was going
in a hansom, and he asked if he might come
too—"Give your brother a lift," he said, for the
cabman to hear him.—I was *rusée :* when we
got into Charles Street I suddenly remembered
that Mrs. Lupton would not like it. I insisted on his getting out. I drove down
Queen Street and then up Chesterfield Street
—I passed him again but he never saw me.
I told the cabman to go to Waterloo Place,
and to Waterloo Place he is going. I took
a hint from Mr. Denham, about whose relationship to me I am getting horribly confused, and

stopped him to pick up "my other brother."—
Why don't you speak to me? Do you mind
the lie?'

'I don't mind anything now,' said John,
thawing a little in her sunshiny presence, and
taking her fluttering hand in his; 'have you
been happy all this while away?'

'Am I late?—it seemed endless. Oh! yes,
I have not been bored: I have a lucky con-
sciousness moreover that I have not been dull.
I had always rather be bored than dull: one
can blame others if one is bored, but one
cannot forgive one's self if one is dull!'

'Dull, my star!'

'Behind a fog often enough, without you,'
said the girl gently, her eyes brimming with
tears. 'John, I must buy a veil: I have seen
three people I know already. Is it not extraordinary that one cannot drive a moment
in Piccadilly without seeing three people one
knows—and nearly always just the three
people one would rather *not* see, aren't they?'

John looked out of the hansom: there were
not three people that he knew in all London.

'Where are we going?' he said after a moment.

Waldine's answer came from behind the muff, with which she was shielding her face from the eyes of a familiar friend.

'To a shop where we can get cards and veil and all—a sort of general village shop, like the one at Netherfield Gate! Do you like driving through these streets? I adore it. Look at the lamps; they have hardly been put out for days! We don't live by sunlight here!'

'Don't you?' said John rather foolishly, contemplating what was mere sunlight to him.

'You have not said three words,' she went on quickly: 'say three words to me, you say nothing. I must have you say three words to spoil the sight of those three hideous people!'

'*I love you.*'

Silence; then after a pause. 'I surrender, John, I cannot talk to you: I can write to you, and often when you are away from me I can talk to your ghostly presence hour by hour. But now that you are really here, you are like a weight upon my heart and I—I think—on yours.'

'You will have all life to talk to me in, I trust,' said John.

'I think I shall never utter: don't you see, John, that for us two there is nothing but love? If you were any other man I know, there would be a hundred safety valves of speech; I could let off the steam. But now . . . you would not care to hear about the princess' bonnet or the grand duke's appetite, would you?—and he did not eat prettily, *par parenthèse !*'

John pushed back the offending hat; she had never even observed it. 'I care for nothing here but you, Waldine,' he said:—'I came here to see you and I have seen you. All that you tell me pleases me, because you say it; but the only thing in London that there is for me is yourself. Do you not understand? You have only to be with me for me to be happy: it is not what you say or do that moves me, it is you. Why are you silent now?'

'Oh! go on speaking to me! Do you know what your words are? There is not a fibre in my heart that they do not thrill: I think it is your voice that I love.'

'I hope that it is me that you love, my darling, me and my love of you.'

'It is not that latter, I know; it has nothing to do with it. I love you as one loves fresh air and music, reckless if they have returning love for one or not—never, I fancy, thinking about that at all. It is your voice, your hands, your kisses that I love, that make the world for me.'

'If I were dumb and maimed and absent——'

'Oh don't talk like that! horrible! how can I tell? it would not be you. Absent, yes! I can stand a certain absence . . . would you love *me* if I were maimed and dumb?'

'Better, if better *can* be, but it can't: you are myself for me, Waldine! A man loves himself: he talks about it little, but see the pains he takes to get it happiness: does he love himself less for such troubles as those?— no, but more. It seems to me dreadful, often,

that the only scope for my compassion towards
you is the risk of your love for me.'

'I don't want your compassion : I have
made no sacrifices : I have added you to my
life.'

'But you are going to make them ? . . .'

'Of course ; but *if* I do—or rather *when* I
do—they won't seem sacrifices.   Don't you
see ? when I go to you, I. shall go because I
love you just too well to do without you any
longer.   Why did you put that tone into your
voice ?   Do you think I would ever go back
from my word ?   For one thing only in life I
have complete contempt—for its timidity.   I
have no qualms, all things are for the best.
Love is the best of things ; there is no second
best.'

'You will marry me and share my grooved
career ?'

'I have said it ; I will say it as often as
you will hear me.   You must trust me, John ;
believe me I was born respectable ! cowardice
is a question of breeding.   You have my
word.   Listen !   If I ceased to love you I

would marry you still if you wished it. If you wished it I would even marry you if you ceased to love me—that's harder, but one does not give one's word for nothing, one gives one's worth with it : I have thought out all this. But I have only begun to love you, John ; I shall take all my days to learn the whole lesson ; and you—you have not ceased to love me yet ? I love you far too well to dream that you will cease to love me yet——'

'Not yet,' said John. Again the little word, the great significance, the mutual thrill.

They were driving down Waterloo Place now, and it was darker turning from the glare of Piccadilly ; the cold damp air blew fresh vigour into Waldine's nerves, as if it were a breath of the sea ; she felt her face cool above the throbbing of her frame, like ice on fever ; she stooped it against his shoulder.

'Waldine,' he said, ' when shall it be, this gift of our life to each other ?'

' Oh ! when you will,' she answered ; ' how can I decide ? we must do what is wisest, and you are the best judge of that. It bothers me to make plans, but I shall not quarrel with yours.'

'Let us think,' said John gently, 'where we are.' . . . He set his mind to ponder.

'We are at Howell and James',' she answered quickly, with a sense of relief, 'and we have half an hour's work before us; give the cabman eighteenpence; we will be economical and not keep him; put on as brotherly a look as you can, and follow me!' The audacity that was upon her was like possession.

She bought a veil, for which John madly longed to pay, but the price of which astonished him greatly. She tied it closely over her face and set about the selection of poor Lady Grenvers' New Year emblems as blindfold as fortune. The warmth and comfort of the place was new life to John; starved and frozen as he was, he glowed and thawed; the look of perfect happiness on his flushed face gave it an ideal—almost transparent— beauty. Through her veil Waldine watched him with intense pride. He seemed to her

like a god : the notion that he was straitened
for small change would have been incredible
had it presented itself to her mind; but she
never thought of him as any way dependant.

'Buy me this, John,' she said when the
parcel was completed, with the air of one who
confers a favour.

It was a little scented sachet of white satin
with a rose outside it—not a thing which she
liked even, not a thing that she needed or
on which she could fasten any association
with the day. He bought it with his last
half-crown.

They went out presently into the street; it
was nearly five o'clock. The thickness of her
veil prevented her from feeling chilled; to
John the keen air struck like rain, all saturated
as it was with fog. Strange, for he had never
used to be one to think of weather!

'I must be home soon after five,' said
Waldine ; 'there is a crowd of people coming,
and I have no sort of excuse. We will walk,
John. Oh! it is not like Whiteknyghts
walking, is it ?'

She paced quickly, but it was not fast for him; they had turned southward and went down the broad steps towards St. James' Park. They made their way more slowly along the skirting avenues and by Constitution Hill to Grosvenor Place, for the Green Park was shut; the darkness, the sense of security, the nearness to the beloved combined to Waldine's entire elation.

'That is where the Prince of Wales lives,' she said; 'Mrs. Lupton means him to distinguish me next season. Perhaps next season we shall be settled in the country and I shall have forgotten Marlborough House as much as you will.'

'We have such soft evenings at Netherfield,' said John, 'in summer weather! Ah, love, last summer I did not know that the world had anything like you—is not that strange? There you were all the time growing up for me, and there was I all the time waiting for you; longing often in the fields, those August evenings, for some one different to the girls I saw, to walk with me between the hedgerows or in the cornfields. I used to wonder how I should find the sweetheart I wanted; she seemed a dream. Till I saw you, and then the dream faded suddenly out; because you were so much more fine and fair than the face it held ! How soon you filled my heart—how full you filled it!'

Waldine listened, listened; his voice, with its slight throat sound, deepened from fatigue and vibrating with passion, lulled her into an ecstasy of which their motion through the winter air was like the pulse; she felt as if they throbbed together in the world without volition of their own or individual being.

It was very dark along the lonely road; only a few saunterers, who did not heed them, saw that John had stolen his arm round the girl's shoulder and that she was walking with her head against his breast. Under the pressure of this air, so charged with secrets, he could tell her his at last. He spoke it as proximity made it more clear to his own sense :

'I loved you from the first; I shall love you till I die. My eyes are blind when I do

not see you, my arms empty when they do
not hold you. For my heart you are life and
death, for my soul you are heaven.'

'I cannot stay in London now without
you,' said Waldine after a pause; 'you have
changed it all for me by this one visit. I did
not know it could contain such bliss. Ah!
John, what immense happiness time holds.
Driving sometimes with Mrs. Lupton I have
thought how charming town-life was with its
gaieties, its perpetual occupation! I have passed
by Hyde Park corner and I have seen people
sauntering about and never suspected that the
saunterers might wholly despise the busy
drivers, never thought that I should soon
stroll here with *my* beloved.'

'So this is Hyde Park corner,' said John
as they came out on the bewildering lights.

'Yes! and do you see the fog? we have
hardly felt it—at least I, for you look strangled
—and John, I said that every foggy day I was
at Mr. Denham's disposal to give him my
maternal counsel. Do you recollect? I wrote
to you all about it. Very likely he is waiting

for me now—an idle son with a face full of confessions.'

'Let him wait.'

'For ever and a day! I promise you, now and for always, that whenever I am with him I will think of only you.'

'That's a pretty promise! will you keep it?'

'With my life! . . . Love, *I* must go; it is late and I have no excuse—and *you* must go— just think of it! you have to catch your train; I know there is one about six, but we have loitered here so long you have no time to spare; you must take a hansom.'

'What are you going to do this evening while I am hurrying away from you—so fast —so fast?'

'Only heaven and Mrs. Lupton know; we have to dine out, else I could avoid the rest. And anyway it will be long past ten before you are at home by that slow train; I suppose you *must* go. . . . It is like taking the life out of my body. Write to me when you are gone.'

She tied the veil across her face again—the

face which John had bared to kiss in the
dusky avenues—and they walked silently along
the south side of Piccadilly. The novelty
of being side by side had become suddenly
familiar: they felt as if they were about to
break off a long while of life together. They
threaded the streets · presently, and it was by
the little dark chapel in Curzon Street that at
last they parted. Many a parting, without
doubt, ere theirs had that little chapel shielded,
many a parting has it shielded since, but
seldom one, perhaps, where the usual mood
was so entirely reversed. Of these two beautiful and youthful lovers here the girl had all
the enterprise and ardour of a boy, the man
had all the docile constancy of a woman.
Waldine was in the pause of a crowded life,
even physically fuller than John's. This
violent passion of love was the one peaceful
instant of her day; she was going on from
strength to strength because of it. Well fed,
warm clad, the crimson of superb health stain-
ing her soft lips, she was, as it were, just
wasting a breathing space of existence in

company of the idol she had chosen. As for him, chilled, hungry, choked with unaccustomed poison in the air—every nerve and fibre strained in rapture of earnest, self-upbraiding love— this was the central pang to which all his hopes had rounded. When this good-bye was done he had to get his endless journey over as he best could, and to live by its remembrance tortured with jealous pain till kindly fate might bring him one chance more. And yet the gift was his, for all that the search was hers.

'Say one thing to me, love,' she said, gazing into his dear, tired face with starlike, dewy eyes; 'one word that I may hold within my heart for ever.'

'Remember,' he answered her, 'once more remember this is all to me. Withhold every-thing or withhold nothing now. I give you this last chance. I am not cruel—I can forgive. But choose! Waldine, my queen, in the sight of God above us, are you my wife or not?'

'Yours only, yours ever,' she said in a sigh that was the echo of his breath.

And then he kissed her again. . . .

Ten minutes afterwards he was running, as fast as one can run in London, through drizzling wet to the station; and Waldine, her face only the fairer, her hair only the sleeker, for the damp, was turning to Mr. Denham's confidences, from among billowy sofa-cushions, the inattentive shell of her ear, in which the humming song of contented passion was yet awake like music.

THE END OF BOOK III.

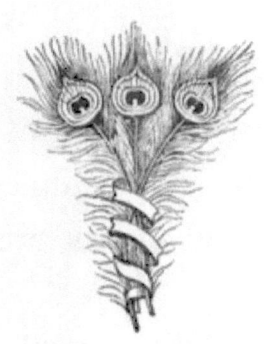

BOOK THE FOURTH

CONTEMPT

'Death looseth'

CHAPTER I.

JOHN LYNE'S LOVE-LETTER

WHITEKNYGHTS COT, *New Year's Eve.*

MY DEAREST GIRL — That is the way that Keats began his love-letters, and I suppose Keats had a sort of notion of the right way. That at least is what you are to me, that and more.

At last I have your leave to write to you— a leave I hardly dare to take. To bring you myself, that is one thing, because you have deigned to accept me, but to bring you my thoughts, that sounds bold.

Yet surely this is the time and this the place, if ever anywhere it can be true that I should write to you as mine.

Waldine, this paper is not worthy of you,

this ink is not clear enough, this pen is not fine enough. Only the hand that guides the pen is *yours enough;* nothing else enough, but yours enough, my dear.

What shall I wish you for the coming year? in an hour or so it will be here, and everything is so quiet and the air so still and keen that I almost fancy I can hear its wings. Perhaps they're the old year's wings, though, that I'm so loth should leave us. Stay a bit, old fellow, you have been the best of friends! But he won't stay: he is going: and what of his successor? I think I'll wish that he may bring you happiness; nothing besides 'matters much,' as you would say.

And you shall give me in return one of your glancing, omnipotent wishes—for health, I think: there is no need for you to wish me happiness; it is in your own gift.

It makes me half ashamed — only that shame is not in love at all—to have to want that you should wish me health. I have been bad again with that same illness, and it's all my own fault. I played the fool by hurrying to the station after our walk together, and got a sort of chill on the journey, after the glow you put in me, I fancy. Anyway it was indoors for me, and no more chances of sporting the London hat—not even for New Year's Day ! All the old trouble of cough and blood-streaks again ; and it goes on still, though lessened.

And his lordship is ill, and chafes for me to go to him ; and they say her ladyship is almost always in her rooms, for fear of draughts,— and—well ! you see, in fact, we want you back again to put our lives to music !

For me you are health and summer : I have no comparisons for your presence ; but when I shut my eyes and think of you it is as if a lilac bush in spring were in my room, and on every bough of it a bird were singing.

You have never seen this room ; it's very simple. I wonder what you would do with it if you had it to alter—that passes all my guessing. It's my bedroom ; and it's got a nice window with a red curtain, now pulled back to show the moonlight : and what besides ? a table and an arm-chair—that's newly added—and a bit of carpet, on which Sep—that's short for September—Sep, my collie, Flirt's successor, is asleep before a bright fire.

And here's me, a poor sick fellow that loves you—that last quality seems to dignify me to my self—in an old shooting-coat and with an old pipe for all companion, which, by the way, I've let go out already thinking of you.

Me, Waldine, me, what am I ? Just your slave; but none the more merry for being such a wholly useless slave just now. If I were a poet, or a bit of a writer of any sort, I shouldn't mind it so much. But this letter when it's written will be the longest piece of writing I've ever done, by a great deal, if I say half that's in my heart to say.

Are you tired of it already ? Oh! I'm not without qualms. How am I to interest you ? I only know one subject of very great interest, and that's a subject you ought to know a good deal more about than I do, because, my love, it is your own dear self. But the qualms are in absence only; when I am with you I have

none.   It seems to me then that I can make
your life.   My love is like a deep well; when
I get outside of myself to see it I am struck
by its small surface, but when you sound it I
get a hint of its capacity.   All the same it is
you that fill the well.   Till you filled it
with the water of love and the light of life it
was merely a hole in my heart.

That was what ached for emptiness those
summer evenings.   Sometimes I have stretched
myself along the grass, almost in physical pain
—for what ?   I did not know then ; it was
only an immense desire of something vague,
which something vague has shaped itself to
palpable you.

Now the fulness of the well, how to bear
it ?   Now the answering arms, how to support
the embrace ? how to wait for it, how to claim
it ?   Love, who knows all these things but
Love, whose moods they are ?

Those lonely summer evenings, how in-
definite, how hazy they were ! to-night how
changed the sky !   I wish you could have
seen the sunset.   We have winter—arctic

winter—a black frost, not a breath of mist, not a trace of fog from morning to morning, absolute crystal clearness in which sun and moon are plain to see and stars are intimate lamps. One feels one could blow them out, if the revelation did not hold one's breath. I get up and go to the window—was it hours ago that sunset flamed itself away in saffron and purple and gold? Hours or centuries was it? What has this deep heaven to do with that burst of passion? Oh Love! the depth of this dark canopy, the calm and silence of it which are not death's calm or silence because of the pulsing stars. Oh Love! the glory of the risen moon, which was so faint and pale in the flooded sunset sky.

It will pass, this fiery insupportable hour which shakes our senses till we hardly discern life's full moon dawning for the flush of marriage saffron all around. Our heaven will darken, deepen, grow more mystical and still.

And then the silver light. Waldine, I have not much to give you: I bring you a

night of stars!   Let the crescent sail in it till
it reach the perfect round.

That's what it seems to me, the life I offer
you—a night of stars.   Will it content you,
sweetest, best, and least considerate of self,
after the garish sky?

Oh! but the worst of it is this, you ought
to look for noontide, not for moonlight.   My
heart misgives me that the sky so bright above
you now is really not sunset's but dawn's.

What if I shall have spoilt your day?
What if my silver moon and quiet starry night
should find you cold, regretful ever of a van-
ished morning?

Already you have spoken me my word of
comfort.   You said you had no fears; you
would own to no regrets.   It was easier to
speak in simile—it seemed to shield my poor-
ness from myself—but that won't do.   Let
me show you what it is that we have done.

We have plighted ourselves to each other
for life or death.   We shall live always in the
same house, we shall lie for ever in the same
grave.   If my station be low, if my grave be

far away, your station and your grave must be with mine. Be *certain* that the great glory that this holds for me holds no reverse for you. I think we could not live here : *that* you will not mind, but realise it once for all. Our place would be anomalous. Will you come with me abroad ? Whither you will ; for me it need not be far, I have so few acquaintances that I need avoid ; but what of you ? I do not want to weary you with details, but what could I do in Europe ? I am the merest Englishman. I think our home must be American, or in Australia. I do see somehow there a sphere for me with my bounded knowledge, a possible wide, happy life for you with your boundless courage and love. Rustic life—almost wild.

Details I will not give you : if you realise this, you will not want to be precise about the where. I will find out all about that. Then comes the when ? Life is not long : will you not marry me soon, my love of loves ? My people are old and well cared for : they have plenty for their lives laid by : I have been

independent of them for some time past,
saving my means. And mine is yours. Yes,
I have the wings to take us, have you the will
to fly? Lark, nightingale, dove, what bird
are you that you will make your nest with a
poor daw like me?

Wife, does it vex you to think that we
must go so far? Oh! it is lucky you are young:
surely you are quite free? London has no
links for you yet, the country-side no chains.
We will forge links and chains out there which
would make the desert home. Now is the
moment. Let us forestall time and death!

Come back, and let us speak about it in this
frost until we make the snow thaw with our
promise : we will talk it over all the spring,
and let us go from summer to summer and
find next December an Australian June.
'You ought to go a sea-voyage,' the doctor
said this morning ; 'you would shake off this
illness altogether so.' And saying it he turned
my heart over in my body with a bound.
Let me build the scheme! Say you 'yes.' I
ask no more counsel. Come summer noon,

come winter night, no weariness, no chill shall ever reach you. Through my brain first must pass any shadow that shall fall upon your eyes, through my breast force its way any pang that shall stir your breath to sighing.

I am between you and the world henceforth. You must peep at it over my shoulder. *My* view of the world? Oh love, my world is you!

Your faithful lover,

JOHN.

Midnight.—There go the bells! my life upon your faith.

God bless you, my darling.

CHAPTER II.

WALDINE'S REPLY

CURZON STREET, *January 2nd.*

'YES!' you ask it: I say it. 'Yes' with shut eyes and fingers in my ears, 'yes' vigilant and listening. Why are you troubled? why do you make plans? I have no troubles and I make no plans. I take you, you take me: all will be well.

And seriously, my own (my very own I know for time and for eternity), I am not wholly irresponsible. I have a sense of honour: you seem to think I haven't! In other senses I *am* wanting, I have no sense of distance. England, Italy, Australia—*where* that latter is I am most uncertain; but anyway the three countries are under one sun, in one air—better air or worse—and for me they hold, or may hold, but one presence. I have a sense of hurry though : don't hasten things ! I mean don't hasten great things : hasten your coming or my going—our meetings and our partings shall be how or where you will. But why disturb a current of existence that can be as calm as ours ? Do you want to leave Whiteknyghts and your people and my uncle ? why should you ? See my prudence : it is obviously,—nay ! it is inevitably, right.

First of all you have to get well. It sounds rather dreadful, but your illness is perfectly intolerable to me. What's the use of chopping words ? I who greatly desire to tell you everything that befalls me, should I not tell you first what I *must* have. I must have you well again, John, well without more delay. Don't think either that I grieve because this illness is, as some would say, my fault. Honestly, it is *not* that which grieves me. It is this : the first thing that I ask of you is health ; devotion afterwards, but capacity before all else. You must bury sickness with the buried year : 'alms for oblivion,' John, you must put weakness into 'Time's wallet.' You will not disappoint me ?

And you must try and be practical—reasonable first and practical next. Dearest, I have a new cream satin dress.—(Oh! there is something of my aunt in me, and I never knew it!)—It was not made for the backwoods. By and by I will dress myself in serge or print—nay, in sackcloth for your sake : but *with* a new cream satin from Elise and *with* you at my side—for what is that path across the park when I am once at home?—why should I not enjoy the pride of both?

How you have made me argue! and it is all such a trifle : you trust me, do you not? you are not jealous? Well then do not be impatient! do not spoil tranquil ease by a snatch at ecstasy with risk. Let us have 'peace with honour!'

These last words have made me laugh. They read as if I did not wish to be your wife! I have no wish in life but that : it ends up all my plans. But it *ends* them : the plans beyond are yours. Do you not understand? Once given, I lose myself, and rightly. If I could think for one instant that you doubted me when I say solemnly that I love you, then —illogical as it sounds—I would marry you to-morrow! But you cannot doubt my love for you any more than I doubt yours for me. And I do not doubt that at all; did not doubt it before I had your letter, do not doubt it now.

Your letter! all this while I have not praised it: I have no words of praise. Dear, one who loved you less might praise it more than I.

There I stop short—because—because I do not want to be ambiguous. I will not have you think I cannot praise it because I am too much moved. The reason, the real reason is that it does not wholly please me. To think that I should be so difficult!

Once I said to you I was not absolutely certain that I wished you to love me. Of one thing I am quite certain: I do not want you overmuch to express your love. I want you in my life for many reasons, but the chief reason is for repression of myself. Let *me* be the fluent speaker—it is so easy. Be you the limitless and throbbing silence. Close up my chattering day, voiceless interpreter ! . . .

Oh me ! choosing all these fine terms, am I still afraid of being truthful ? Is the real fact merely that your way of speaking is not what I would have it be ? Is your letter, despite its devotion, or *because* of its devotion, a sort of weariness ? I would to God I knew. . . .

John, don't look hurt ! you would not dream that I am careless of your love if you could see me now. I have perused your letter twenty times : I have no fault to find with it. But, dear, it does not stir my depths as your long silence stirred them. Mine be the blame of this ! But you must know the case : then you shall write or not write as you will. I love you with my whole heart, I am not sure that I love you with one lobe of my brain. I would let my heart, set free, win the conversion of my mind.

Enough: my reasoning is all abroad. Only, once more, don't try to utter fancies : I credit you with the unutterable always. Just tell me common facts, if needs be, dates and hours. What you are to me, have you any notion? I have no words to tell it you ; but, whatever it is, it is my heart has made you this for me. Yet what you did not make, you somehow still might mar. Can you understand this ? It is simple.

I must try and frame it rationally to your knowledge. A certain outside self of me is more the slave of things usual than I thought. I have speeches made to me all day by one and the other, with which I do not want to put your speech into comparison.

It would be like your coming up to London without a high hat : I don't know why, but it would : remember you were a shock to me then! I have not quite got over it yet !

Be my compass, my mainspring, my prince, my life, my god ! But, for your own sake, lift me up to you, do not come down—such a descent it is !—to me.

There! I am ill to-night. Surely it must be illness that makes a woman misprise herself. Shall I diagnose my illness for you as you do for me that most vexatious one of yours? I have discussed it with Mrs. Lupton, and she says it is ambition. For my part I call it fatigue. She says I want an embassy, I say I want rest.

Oh! is the secret to be solved by double life? I wonder.

To be happy I desire power, but I desire a slavery therewith: I have the longing to rule a kingdom, but be ruled by you. Perhaps sex is my trouble; if I were a man I could lead two lives; and why not now? Why try to run a complex personality in a single groove?

Don't think I hesitate or balance any choice whatever in my mind. I don't: I have chosen you; I have foregone success, so called. And yet, so far as this success may be compatible with your possession of me, I want you to let me taste it. Let me know the worthlessness of the sphere that I resign before I resign it in your favour. A concession like this will be generous.

Very often it seems to me, John, that I love you as a man loves a woman. I adore your beauty, I hold my breath before your gentleness. I know no sweetness upon earth like the sweetness of your kiss. But your protection—do I want that? Oh! no a thousand times; it only makes me smile. You say that you will shield me; but then I have no wish to be shielded—

> '. . . in me si muove
> Un anima selvaggia.'

You have not forgotten your Italian?—'selvaggia,' yes! that's it. I am Waldine, to change the sense a little. I ask for choice, to choose you always in the end, but to be forced to decide. How else is there action in life, how else is there worth in love? Dear, don't talk of protecting me—a gun can do as much; don't talk of providing for me—a fool can do more! Draw out my tears with your tenderness, draw out my soul with your voice. That is your province. As to the world and the world's value, I need no help, no added courage, to make me face the one or despise the other.

A thousand pardons! I ask your pardon always, I know not why. But one thing in me needs neither forgiveness nor concessions, the truth I show you. Is not my truth a merit? Yet not mine, but yours. For yours I am, to take or leave, yours for all claims and all time. And shall I not be true? 'Oh yes!' you answer, and your tone, unheard, thrills me although you are so far away :—'Oh yes! it is surely best for both of us that you should be true!' I will.

Was that a sigh of yours, my love, that closed the whisper and seemed an answer to my breath of relief?—for confession is over: I have nothing more that is hard to tell you, all is said and done. I do not want to hear you sigh like that, when I am alone with you, like this, of evenings.

For indeed, indeed, you are here! Wherever I may be now — at home, abroad, in shops or theatres — I hold you in my heart : you are my talisman against another care. I cannot think of any shame or any sorrow that one instant of your embrace would not blot out from me for ever. Strange gift you give me, absolute intoxication of sense!—and then to attempt speech of it! No, no, we shall express things sometime, but not now.

You are ill, you say. How to amuse you? Mrs. Lupton or Lady Grenvers could amuse you better than I. Love makes me sad, exacting, cross: it is an enervating mist about me. . . . Ah! by the way, John, it is strange that the only two women I should have seen intimately since I came to England should guide me— little dreaming it—more and more straight to you. My aunt is incarnate vanity. Her influence has been to set me against self. I am wholly sickened of her care for her beauty and her dress. She presents what she would call mere rustic slavery, by contrast, in its most attractive form. Her introspection (let me frame it philosophically if I can) moves me to expansion the more. Because of her prevailing powder-puff, I pine for sun-tan and freckles.

Mrs. Lupton's influence has been more dangerous than this incitement by opposites : she has roused my daring. John, I do not believe in all Mrs. Lupton's adventures, but I have got to feel it is my mission to prove them possible. I furnish the examples to her text of life. It was her fault at first : it will be her fault still until her fancy fails her. She is not more than a dreamer; but I have lived her dream. She often says to me, *not*, I now believe, from her own experience, ' We modern women must keep life and love apart.' And then I come straight to you and say to you, ' We have fulfilled Mrs. Lupton's ideal in many ways : let us fulfil it also in this.'

For a time ! For a time only. I ask you but a breathing space. And, dear, how charged with sweetness will be the air we breathe the while ! My wish is this :— for you are right that I cannot stay a great while longer away.— Let me return and let us live our daily life, glorifying ever what moments of it you will, by meetings at your pleasure.

While I am here I am amused—I confess it; there would be almost cause for you to be jealous if you saw my surroundings. But at Whiteknyghts! you will not grudge me my uncharmed moments there. There is no one— scarcely any one, is there?—that will come as far as Whiteknyghts to find me, of all my London friends. I will test them at any rate. 'If they should come?'—you say. Oh! but they won't.

I had a hundred things to say to you, but they are too trifling. All that matters really in what I have written is the news that I am coming. Early, very early in this young year, I am coming, to find the one real passion the world holds for me.

Answer me in a word, you perfect lover! Shall I not come? shall it not all be as I will? I sail upon the clouds in expectation: do not make me feel myself only ballooning by the suggestion of any chain to earth however silken. Raise your spirits to my level! Meet me up here in heaven! . . .

A shiver brings me back to earth—a shiver like an omen of evil. The fire is out. My ecstasy seems to have passed. I am,—once again,—your poor, perplexed

WALDINE.

CHAPTER III.

AN AFFIRMATION

COME then, my dearest, when you will, and let us lead. what life you choose together. Half together, if not yet wholly; but not apart, as now, again.

My last qualm is against letting any words bind you. For you would always speak the more generous resolve. I will let only your action bind you past recall. If you come to me now, you come as my promised wife. Whether our wedding day be in summer or winter does not seem to me to matter. You know what you do.

But, once returned here, whether your home be at this side of the world or at the other, you are mine : there is to be no going back.

I was to give you facts. My father is ill. He has had an accident: and my mother is worn out with watching him. Think of me as better, watching too. But it is only half my sight that watches the old man's sleep; and the more wakeful half watches the road for you.

My child, my mistress! it costs me something to leave the paper blank. And yet I know how poor my words must seem to you. Look into my heart: I'll warrant you will not be disappointed there.

JOHN LYNE.

CHAPTER IV.

LITTLE FOXES

'I HAVE not,' said Mrs. Lupton, summing up, as was her wont, an article of her negative creed for Waldine's behoof, 'any opinion at all of my own sex.'

It was an interval in the busy London day, that opportune moment preceding tea (and the inevitable tea-side danglers) which she was fond of improving before she launched into her airy cynicisms. It was a moment full of memories for Val; it was for just this hour she had walked with John Lyne on Constitution Hill.

'Your mood is Delphic,' she answered absently, 'and that gray velvet gown is *tomb-y*, as Aunt Linda would say. Utter, my oracle, and tell me why?'

She sat herself at Mrs. Lupton's feet; she experienced always now a longing for caresses. She put her head on Mrs. Lupton's knee, Mrs. Lupton stroked it with her small nervous hand which felt the softness of the hair without divining a throb of the brain.

'Of you, my dear, I have a sort of notion, but the most of us are quite elusive; one must mistrust us, because trust has no foundation. Oh! I don't mean that I have a bad opinion of women. I mean just what I say— I have *none* — we are such a menagerie. Worldly women are like turkeys and tortoises. If you don't strut and gobble, and fatten your body and wrinkle your face, you must get a shell and creep about beneath it. Ethelinda has become a tortoise already; her shell is self, and how she polishes that shell! I shall be a turkey, Val, I know it. I have shuddered at Christmas fare like a cannibal, and I suppose that's the reason. Oh! the want of courage that sends us all to the same farmyard or floor. We who thought once to fly, in the end we waddle or crawl.'

'I suppose I shall finish as one or the other,' said Val laughing, 'tortoise or turkey, shall I crawl or gobble?—But I always thought Aunt Linda was a butterfly.'

'It *is* the butterfly, dear, that swells and hardens into the tortoise; I have watched it often. For myself I have prayed to be neither tortoise nor turkey, yet I often feel the clutter in my throat and I know my doom. But widowhood helps me,' she concluded with a sigh :—'Be a widow, Val! It is difficult, but I don't see why it should be impossible to forecast it, if you choose your man.'

'Think of some other mode of emancipation,' said Waldine slowly, repressing an odd shiver :—'I want an original life.'

'*A* life,' Mrs. Lupton echoed; 'we always say "*a* life," as if it were a certain line of tram or railway. Yet Chance is still standing by us with hands full of varied hours: the thing is to get a safe foothold within reach of them. I have made my perch; it is not lofty, but it is easy; thence I select samples of existence.'

'Samples would not suffice me; I am more robust than you. I want to lose myself.'

'Inartistic; in fact coarse! I am convinced of the need for a safe critical standpoint. There shall Chance toss you the hours: play with them what game you will and let them fall, but keep your foothold. By the way, Waldine, you must marry soon.'

'Indeed, ma'am, and why?'

'For a reason the reverse of the common; most women marry for protection, you must marry to protect. Your husband must be perpetually drawing out your masculine qualities, and you will find the feminine virtues increase with the demand.'

'That's obscure; but if I understand you, I think you are right about me.'

'What a grave tone! . . . Mr. Denham? Ah! you have precluded a confession! I was going to put some home-questions to Waldine: and she would have responded . . . who can prophesy how? Likely enough, in Chinese fashion, by more questions! So that it's as well you came. But answer, is the fog really thick enough to warrant your being admitted again to-day ?'

'It is black out of doors,' said Mr. Denham sheepishly, 'I took for granted that it was fog.'

Waldine had not risen ; she was still gazing steadily into the fire. He came across to shake hands with Mrs. Lupton and then stooped over her ; she took his hand, but it was only to raise herself from the floor. When she had done that, she walked away a step or two, regardless of his having pressed her fingers. She did not even say 'thank you' for his assistance.

Mr. Denham looked at her ; she wore a simple gown of a sort of soft dark fleece ; her head showed above it like a flower out of brown mould. Her face had the sort of vividness that pales paint. Coming in from the cold air, she had fluffed her cheeks with rice-flour a little, and a few grains of it rested upon the ivory and rose of her beauty like an earthy stain. The texture and tint of her skin were alike so lovely that the least artificial touch disfigured them. She was standing near a lamp, the light from which, diffused through a white paper shade, was full upon her hands as she tied and untied a long brown ribbon knotted in a loose bow upon her bosom. Her hands were like lilies.

Mr. Denham looked at her. She was to him an enchantment, a mystery, a goddess. Mrs. Lupton looked at Mr. Denham and smiled; he was not even a riddle to her.

'You have no news,' she said in rather a meaning voice.

'No,' he answered, 'you always know everything first. I've nothing to tell you.'

His tone, which he made purposely impressive, attracted Waldine's attention.

'How comes it you remain in town?' she asked him; 'I thought you were devoted to hunting.'

'Oh! I like London too,' he answered, awkward and crimson; 'I shall stay up some time.'

'Shall you?' she said; 'I confess I don't care for it any more. I would say so to no hostess but Mrs. Lupton; she permits whims:

and if I don't like it under her auspices I should like it less under my aunt's. I have a caprice for isolation, my palate is cloyed with pleasure.'

'Yes, there *is* too much pleasure,' said the Hon. Launcelot sadly, 'but I should have thought you found Whiteknyghts dull.'

'I adore dulness,' said Waldine—'dulness, cold, loneliness : I want the tonics of these. I feel like a Skye terrier that has been kennelled in a hothouse.'

'But surely Whiteknyghts is like a hothouse quite as much ?'

'I suppose it is not perfect,' she answered impatiently, 'but attending perfection—that's a French phrase I fear—it pleases me well enough.'

'You like that part of the world ?'

'Sufficiently well '—she stopped short and put one of her white hands to her head. There had darted through her mind like a swift pain the vision of that adorable wild land about Whiteknyghts which was covert to the only quest she sought.

'You would not hate to make it your home?' His tone was a little anxious now.

'It *is* my home: you are like Magnall's questions, only not so well worded. . . . Look at Mrs. Lupton's visitors, they are more amusing than I am.—Who is that?'

'It is Lady Trefusis; is she not handsome?

'Eugenia Trefusis! the one woman Mrs. Lupton loves. Let us sit down here and you shall tell me about her.'

'All the world knows: "She is as good as she is beautiful," et cetera. None the less I believe she was once passionately in love with a brute called Jarvis. Mrs. Lupton knows him too.'

'That dreadful Captain Jarvis who rides in the row with Mrs. North?'

'The same; the man who married Miss Buxton.'

'I think I can understand the infatuation.'

'You?'

'I. Don't look so horrified; I do not know him, and I have only seen her in the distance. I may be wrong; but I realise the

position. Captain Jarvis was the unknown
for Miss Brand; she had no landmarks. Had
she been less angelic she would have been
much harder to deceive.—Does she ever see
him now?'

'Never. She has set up the landmarks
with a vengeance since.'

'That also I can understand. What a face
she has! she makes Mrs. Lupton look like a
wicked doll. I suppose everybody in London
has a history.'

'Everybody one knows, I should think.
Why that serious look? Do *you* want a
history?'

'I don't know what I want: I want to
stand bareheaded in the rain—that first.'

'It's the heat of the room.—Miss de Stair,
will you let me tell you what it is you want?
I am the sort of fellow that is very little good
at words, and one does not make speeches
nowadays, you see; but I think what you
long for is to have your own way in everything, and what I wish is that you would let
me help you to have it.'

'I don't know that you are right, and I don't see how you can help me.'

'Don't you?' he laughed nervously, changing colour a little, under her steady stare, but man enough all the while not to flinch from his position.—'You might at least let me try. It is like this. As things are, you have nothing to gain by anything you may do. But if you were—different, in different circumstances—everything you did would matter, and not to yourself alone.'

'We none of us live to ourselves alone,' said Waldine with mock solemnity :—'Have you any notion how ridiculous you look lecturing me? Your face is quite red and the collar of your coat is on end with excitement. I never knew men's clothes were sympathetic—wool to the sheep.'

'You are not kind,' said the young man, dumfoundered at her rudeness :—'But have *you* any notion how beautiful you look when you laugh? yes, and when you frown too? I wish I had your photograph like that.'

'Photographs are vulgar things. Mrs.

Lupton and I had a perfect holocaust yesterday; we burnt you in effigy I can't tell you how often; it's a marvel that you have survived it. You will have to present her with at least a dozen new ones to fill the empty frames.'

'I have had some new ones taken; may I give you one? if so Mrs. Lupton may have the rest.'

'I suppose you may; but I shall not frame it.'

'You will not burn it?'

'No, I will take the greatest care of it: I will put it away in a box, lock the box and throw away the key.'

'Well, as you will. What sort of copy shall I send you? they're wonderful fancy affairs, my new photographs; plain or embossed?'

'I should think the plain ones would be the most like you,' said Waldine carelessly: and then they both laughed, like children, and he could not press his suit.

But having silenced him, she returned, womanlike, to the dangerous ground.

'This repartee was but an interlude,' she

said, leaning back in her chair; 'you were teaching me my London. Lesson the first, to disbelieve everything; I cannot skip so soon to lesson the last, to believe in you. Tell me; it does not trouble you that people have had histories?'

'I should have very little sleep at nights if it did.'

'And you sleep well after the " fitful fever " of your days?'

'Like a dog; nobody's scrapes bore me; even my own don't keep me awake.'

'Have *you* had " a history ? " '

He blushed. 'No—yes! I suppose so, a hundred—nothing considerable.'

'Novelettes at most, or shall we say paragraphs?'

'Oh! I'm not worth discussion; and I believe in fresh starts up to a certain age.'

'For a woman also? May I have novelettes and paragraphs?'

'You are like nobody else. How am I to tell you what I think about women? They must be very young to start quite fresh . . .

but what do you know ? And I—Miss de Stair,
the feminine world divides itself for me into
" you," and " other women." '

'That is a very pretty speech, I suppose ;
I am vain enough to take it so.'

'It is meant to be. You see for *me* you
can't do wrong. Even when you are hard on
me it seems all right. There is nothing I could
not forgive you, nothing I could not excuse
you. . . . Because I want you so. Oh ! won't
you let me tell you how much I want you ?'

His voice had become quite thick with
emotion ; its low, deep tone, because it did
not melt her in the least, froze Waldine's confidence—she was half frightened, half amused.

'Don't go on talking now,' she said, pushing her chair aside a little :—'Open the door
for Lady Trefusis and bring me some toast.'

The wonder in her heart was answered!
She could envisage choice. From what worse
evil should one pray to be delivered ?

CHAPTER V.

THE WORLD WELL LOST

AND it was with the knowledge that she left a lover, still undeclared, in London, that Waldine de Stair returned to Whiteknyghts soon afterwards. Returned to havoc, sorrow, pain—to the undisguised seams of life. Returned gladly: she was independent of them all.

Her latter days in town had been days of almost unmixed pleasure, but she had not enjoyed them at the time. Her heart's blood had absorbed the poison of London variety and London insincerity without her knowledge, but the poison left no immediate trace upon her will. Because still superbly potent above it was the desire of love.

She came back to the country like a freed prisoner: her young step bounded up the broad, still staircase, whispered, rather than echoed, along the warmed corridors, was music to Lord Grenvers, and to her ladyship not seldom perplexity and fear.

'Don't *bounce* into the room, darling,' she said at last, when surprised in too flagrant self contemplation with the familiar hand-glass: ' Never *bounce* or *steal*. *My* way of entering the room has been so much to my poor saint for years. It's not that I don't want you always, but my nerves are so sensitive. I really should have thought your long visit to Charlotte would have taught you . . . poor Charlotte ! I never dared enter *her* room without knocking, or even go round the corner without a cough; but she was younger then ! . . . I suppose *now*. . . . And that was different ! By the way, I have never seen a woman let her complexion *go* as Charlotte has done—not that it ever was much—still *pea-soup*, really *pea-soup*. My face is a *disease* to what it was— yes ! Val, a *disease*—but it *is* human flesh.'

'There are other things in the world beside complexions,' said Waldine; but her ladyship did not attend; she was mounted on her favourite hobby of self and self's demands.

'What was that tiresome game one used to play?' she went on in a slow, sad voice, absently taking up the hand-glass again. '"Animal, vegetable, or mineral,"—that was it. Some women look vegetable or mineral—now I *am* animal still.'

'You are ethereal,' said the girl laughing. Lady Grenvers heard that; her ears contained some special valve for compliments, which was always open. They entered in and dwelt there.

'You spoil me, Val,' she said, 'but every one has always spoiled me! No, dear, I am *animal*,—a poor worm of course, but not a potato or a lump of lead; *you* are animal too, Val; your complexion is almost too—too, what is it?—violent. I hope you won't get apoplectic by and by.'

'I hope not,' said Waldine—'yes, Aunt Linda, I suppose I am. Animal? Human?

Well! who would really care to be a stone or a soul?'

'Horrid!' said her ladyship, putting a period to the discussion with her usual comment as soon as she was out of her depth.

Were they stones or souls — Waldine wondered—the people about her? or were they just half-people or were they dead? She went to the window and looked out from its one unmuslined square—a white world, with black, snow-fraught sky above it; somewhere he was waiting for her now. Was it cold? was that the whimper of the wind across the park? she did not care.

'I think I shall go out for a run,' she said at last, her tentative tone anticipating a rebuke. '"The snow lies white," but we may be quite snowed in to-morrow.'

'Ah! what a pretty song that was. *I* used to sing it. "The snow lies white."' Lady Grenvers hummed it to herself over the hand-glass, which reflected to her that the powder 'lay white' also.

Waldine waved her a kiss and left her. She preferred the snow for choice.

There was a sort of fire alight in the girl's senses. The icy airs crept round her in vain; the frost only dared the blood to her feet and hands; nothing chilled her. Nor was it only love that warmed her through. She was in supreme and ardent health; her restful life of luxury made her impervious to fatigue or weather. She was more hardy than her lot in society demanded; she had a reserve of energy and warmth. Why waste it here?

She fastened some furs round her neck and put on a velvet hat; then she glided out of the door and breathed the fresh wind, crystal clear, across the waste land and the snow. It was a fairy scene. To her, so newly steeped in London fog and gaslight, the purity of this rare atmosphere, the visible descent of gradual night were boons that brought intensity of feeling and succinctness of resolve. As she stepped quickly over the iron fields, crunching the drift like salt, her thoughts were travelling wind-swift in her brain.

'Is that the world?' she said aloud, 'for which so many people dare and bear so much? I have heard Aunt Linda quite envied: there has never been any scandal about her; women would give their lives to have her wealth, her reputation, and her husband's love: and yet the centre of her being, where does one find it? In that little ivory knob by which she holds her powder-puff! It is there.'—She laughed, but not unkindly, and kicked the snow as if it were the orris root and violet meal she scorned.

—'And Mrs. Lupton's world! it is quite as trivial really—her life is a twirling toy; she can stop it and no one will mind; she can change it and only rest people's attention. It does not *do*. Does anything *do* on earth, I wonder, that has no claims and brings no suffering? I had rather have my uncle's life than hers.'

Her thought saddened as it traversed Lord Grenvers' sphere; she walked more slowly and in silence; after a moment she smiled. She was thinking of Mr. Launcelot Denham.

Simply by contrast! Illness connotes health and suffering strength. It was no treasonable thought; he meant to have the good things of the world; he meant to make a life. So far very well. But he had made his world spin and his life hang on her will and from her finger. And for her, his world with every other world, his life with every other life, were so well lost for love.

Love, incarnate and her own, that was waiting for her under the bare ash-tree boughs! She had met John every day since her return; she had been building busily at that imaginary dwelling-place wherein their twin souls were some time to dwell. And here the tree was, full in sight, and he had not failed her yet.

Her glance was too impassioned now, and too possessive, to note that he was changed. Not less handsome, not less radiant,—taller he looked indeed,—but he had lost flesh, and the brightness of his eyes burned over hollower cheeks; the voice in which he greeted her was deeper than of old, had husked its ringing tone, more muffled day by day.

'Ah!' he said, 'you have come at last. Kiss me once, twice; Waldine, I have heavy news.'

'Do not tell it me yet! Let me be a little glad of your presence first.'

To be with him was an enchantment to her, to be in his arms an ecstasy; she launched herself upon the tide of love like a boat on summer waves. For him too her kiss was an intoxication, an oblivion. . . . They made June in winter.

'What is your bad news?' she asked him at length, smiling up into his face.

He sighed. 'Nothing hurts you that I can tell you, does it?' he said with tender care.

'Nothing; my only suffering is when I am absent from you; then it aches here like hunger.' She put his strong bare hand upon her heart. Its beating sent the colour to his cheeks and lips—the beating of the heart that made his joy.

'Oh!' he said softly, 'do not make me too happy to-day. Waldine, my father is dead.'

The words had little meaning for her; she had never known his father; she had not allowed herself to think ever about his parents except as people that must die some day—unwelcome figures that would yield the stage at last.

She pressed him closer in her arms, with a sweet gravity of look that soothed him like music. She took him away from life and, in the new world that she made for him, she asked him the very truth.

'It is soon,' she said—'sudden rather. John, are you very sad—very sorry? Should you not have minded this much more a year ago? Tell me "yes"!'

('A year ago!' How could he remember what he would have minded then?)

'There is no blank you cannot fill for me by one dear word,' he answered. 'But each sad circumstance, each loss that comes to me, will be a wound until you heal it.'

'Tell me about his death,' said Waldine quickly, with evasive eyes. She looked across his shoulder, she saw the long cold stretch toward his home: she sighed.

'It is good of you to look sad,' he said, 'it
is good of you to sigh. No! why should I
tell you? He died this morning, without any
pain, from some brain injury he got in the
fall. He was an old man, sweetheart; you
are right: I will not be sorry. But I am
troubled about my mother: can you guess
what the loss of him is to her?'

'I think so. If I thought I should be any
good, I would come with you to see her.—
Perhaps you wished it? Yes;—but not just
yet. I cannot act; and I have no personal
affection for her. Your people were not dear
to me because of you, as they would have
been to some women. They were only people
who had a certain claim upon your love and
upon your time. I have resented them
always.'

'You are so strange, Waldine; sometimes
I think you are made of marble and sometimes
of fire.'

'Common hard stone, call it, for the rest:
mere flame for you—you are not so wholly
wrong. Dearest, be rational! I see precisely

how things stand. You have thought to
yourself:—" Why, here is her moment! She
will come and throw herself upon my mother's
neck and be a daughter to her from henceforward." But that is just what I could never
do. If I went with you now I should either
patronise her or alarm her. Let her consola-
tion be that you are still hers for a time.—
Ah! not for long.'

'But by and by?'—said John, doubtful
though half convinced against his will.

'By and by she will die too,' said the girl
impatiently, 'she is not immortal. Oh! love,
don't look so shocked: don't say I give you
more sorrow! But can't you see that your
mother and I should not agree under one roof?
Can't you see, John, that your isolation is the
one thing that makes you possible? You
have kept yourself apart from the rest to some
good end, but you must be isolated wholly.
I shall give up my world for you, but you
must give up yours for me. And death ends
ties so gently and so well. Oh! I believe in
death. See! it is not a doom apart: we

must all die to make way for progress.   Is
not that philosophy?'

'It may be so: 'tis a new view of death
for me.'

'"There are no fields of amaranth on this
side the grave,"' she said, '"there is no name,
with whatsoever emphasis of passionate love
repeated, of which the echo is not faint at
last." That is Landor's: if I could speak such
honey, it is that I would have said. You
must lose me sometime, or I must lose you:
or if we kill ourselves together the rest of the
world must lose us. Some day we must lose
each other! It is written. Not to miss our
happiness while we have it in hand: that is
what matters. Beloved, I resist no longer.
The resolve your news brings me is that I will
marry you to-morrow if you will. I accept
your father's death, not for hindrance but for
spur. Anybody will look after your mother
till she dies!'

But, Waldine,' said John, in utter dis-
traction of mind, 'what is this that you say?
Do you not realise how this great loss of hers

must bind me—*us*—to my mother? How
can I—we—leave her soon? how can we
leave her ever? You are so—is it un-
English? it cannot be heartless. How shall
I teach you life?'

'*You* teach me life!' she cried. 'Poor John,
it is not life you have to teach me: it is love
—love, as you read it, which indeed I half
approve. I think you love me well, I believe
you will love me for ever. But life! leave
life to me. You asked me to emigrate: had
I gone with you and your father died afterwards, as he must have done, we should not
have returned. I would not go: I wished
things to arrange themselves, links to fall off
and leave our freedom clear: now the first
link has fallen. Let us congratulate ourselves
that we did nothing to force it.'

'What do you mean?'

'Is impatience then a sealed book to you?
Can you not understand the longing to be
free goading one into striking off obstacles,
scattering them to right and left. On my life,
I think such a struggle would fill one's days

far better than laments and lassitude. You
look so struck with fear that I am possessed
with a desire to tell you all my worst. John, I
believe I have no heart except to live by: I
know but one sort of love. Don't you think
I would pitch Uncle Grenvers out of window
—bath-chair and all—and put arsenic into
my aunt's lip-salve, sooner thar let them part
me from you ?'

He smiled at her plain words. 'You are
a tigress, my beauty,' he said with reflected
passion, as he strained her in his arms, the
wild blood wakened in him with her laughter.
But it was not the rose-leaf kiss of old :

'Come with me now !' he murmured.

'Let me go,' she said, still laughing, 'remember
this is your afternoon for sackcloth and ashes,
though it may be also my hour for secret joy.
But I want no secrets from you. John, I
am glad of your father's death, and you must
get over it without my help. Look how dark
it is and feel how cold !' she put her cheek
against his hand.

'Yes, it is cold,' he answered, as he loosed

her :—' Well, what are we to do ?   Love, I am
in your hands : I stop the clock of my old
conscience here.   At first I shall be a bad echo
to your leaps of time ; but teach me plain
what flights to take.'

'I want no flights at present : here we
stand under our own twin tree—my tree : the
one bit of landed property which I possess !
We have youth, health, love—perfect trust.
And I have courage. . . . But it is an odd
sort of courage : it goes from me when you are
not by.   There are times when I feel subject
to any moment's magnetism and capable of any
crime : other times there are when I become
an innocent and happy self.   Have you no
experience of such changes ?'

'I don't think much about them,' said
John humbly, 'I am too simple for you yet :
but I do think, Waldine, that half of your
complexity is youth.   You play ball with life
and death because your nerves are not yet
sensible of weight.   I shall make you so tame,
my darling, by and by.'

'That will be better than my worsening

you!—Oh we have talked into hours, and you are going back to a sad home! Have I no compassion? I ought to be so sorry. Love, I want to see you again to-night: these stars do not shine for nothing. And such a moon, Endymion! Ah! she is in love with you, that foolish moon, to shine upon your face like that.' She took off his cap, and with her arms clasped round his neck, she gazed at his beauty, her whole soul, her whole being, aflame within her burning eyes.

'I will come,' said John, 'if you want to see me: I will walk up at nine o'clock this evening, and stand by the window of your music-room —like last night! like last night.'

'Ah! then I am content: I could not say good-bye. Love, what is that shadow moving down the road?'

'It is a man on horseback coming from the Court: it looks like Mr. Denham.'

'Impossible: he is in London still. I told you—did I not?—that he is in love with me?'

'I knew it. You did not tell me.'

'What a tone! So he is best there, is he not? we do not want him here?'

'Oh Waldine, do not name him! should I ever name another girl to you? Ah! well, I will be silent if you will keep your hand upon my lips like that. Must you go, sweet, must you go? I feel you flutter like a bird within my arms.'

'Now or never. Whisper: you do not mind about your father any more? you love me best? No words: a whisper is too loud: I hear it in your heart.— *Yet—tell me once!*'

He bent his head over her cheek, his mouth to her lovely ear, till her temples flamed at his breath. . . . Who dares give his words? He only knows them who has in such a way, at such an hour, let loose the floodgates of his pent-up soul.

Heart of a woman, filled with that full tide, what in your life is made of the passionate river? Only a draught to quench your instant thirst: only refreshment for bright lips and luring eyes that afterward shall smile and shine upon other waters.

CHAPTER VI.

WALDINE WRITES

WHITEKNYGHTS, *February 7th.*

ELSIE mine, long neglected : lost and found
again, as one loses and finds one's friends, in
the maze of memory, how shall I excuse myself
for your many letters not answered at all, your
many other letters answered by a hurried line ?
Best, I think, by telling you all my news in
this, such as it is to tell.

Remember, dear, I am a rustic now. Do
not expect surprises : and keep yourself prepared for a tone of sadness. I have done with
cities : I want to be a rustic all my life.

This afternoon I have built myself away
from the world : locked doors, closed curtains,
barred shutters : I am going to piece together

my existence for you, to pick up the threads of my loom.   And first you want the figures of the scene.

You will have heard that my uncle is ill : his plight is such that at the time you first heard it probably he was better again : and by the time you heard he was better he was certainly worse.   I caught Aunt Ethelinda the other day discussing widow's weeds with him : what a true disappointment she will feel that he can never see if they become her !   He makes all sorts of preparations for his death : and sets his house in order as a good man should.   I am with him a great deal oftener than I was at first.   My love of the place, which has grown into a passion, pleases him more day by day.   He understands that my aunt will never care to live here without him. I doubt if she knows the landmarks round the first turn in the road or the look from any point of view but her boudoir window : I suppose, after the event she will travel and become the cynosure of continental hotels.   I often wish that you could hear her *crescendo,* with its gradual changes of tone. It commences sadly :

'When my poor saint is gone,' she says, '"gone over to the majority," Val, as the Greeks used to say—I am half a Greek myself since those tableaux—Ah ! *what* is to become of poor Queen Venus ? Everything goes to a cousin or something horrid I have never cared to know : the title is extinct and shoals of females will divide the spoil, so fat and hideous they can only marry into the learned professions —Ichabod ! . . . He leaves me what he can, I believe, but what is money to a widow ? My one comfort is that I shall *never* be a dowager : though with a name like mine—*made* for a dowager—to evade being " Ethelinda, Lady Grenvers," is after all not utterly consoling.'— And then, with rather a more cheerful accent : —'When my poor saint is gone, dear Val, I shall have to travel. Awful, of course, for I am such a stay-at-home ; but I can't help feeling that it will be my only chance. Where shall I go ? some dull place first, I suppose : Venice. But what is the good of crape at

Venice? It does not matter what one wears there : I shall go about in a hat, and lace in the evening. . . . Have you never been to Venice, Val? You shall come with me! I imagine it will be next autumn. At first we shall have to be very quiet, but one may get quite a rest and change there before—well! it will depend on circumstances whether one can go out or not next season. What do you think?' And then she lapses into silence, while the periods of sorrow are reckoned!

And yet, dear Elsie, when the time is come, I know she will be inconsolable; but in the meanwhile she diverts herself with attention divided between schemes of mourning and of *trousseaux*, for she has set her heart upon my marriage.

You have guessed to whom? It is one of those things that seem fated : ever since I came here it has been obvious to the meanest intelligence that sooner or later I must marry Launcelot Denham. And the worst of it is that it seems as obvious to him!

Realise my *entourage!* an aunt whose folly is more magnetic and decisive than another woman's reason; an uncle of superior gifts who approves her judgment in all things; a lover—well! one would not wish a fonder or more earnest lover than the devoted Launce. Why, the sequel of the story is not worth writing! It is a question of date. Give reins to your conception of eligibility—yes! and you may give scope to your fancy too—the real man would not disappoint you. On the face of things it would be impossible to refuse Mr. Denham. Oh! whither will life lead me? I was born to be hanged.

'Flippant,' you say. Remember flippancy with me was always an excuse from tears. But I don't want to discuss my failings with you; I want to give you statements; then you shall mount your tripod and deliver the prophetic roll. You can predict of me with some experience.

I went to London with Mrs. Lupton; Mr. Denham was there. Hardly a day passed but we met; and wherever we might chance to be, he made it plain that there was no one there for him but me. Not unpleasant; there were no exactions; I bade him farewell a free woman, as I am to this day. I returned to Whiteknyghts only glad to leave him in town. He was to remain there some time longer. But he did not do so. Listen.

You know—I do not want to write upon this subject—that I have had a *toquade* for 'the bailiff' here. Do not misinterpret the cool tone of this statement; it is just in this way that I try to formulate the position to myself. Whether I have felt superficially or deeply, whether I have been wise or foolish, these points are incidental, they do not alter the fact. I saw 'the bailiff' in London; up to that meeting he had seemed to me a sort of god; since then he has seemed to me only a rather inexperienced young man. But in my personal regard—is that the term?—for him this made no sort of difference. When I came back here I was honestly glad to see him again—glad with my whole heart. If I could entirely divorce him from surroundings I should be glad to see him all the days of my life. But his surroundings have fatigued me of late. He has lost his father, and his mother

frets herself deathwards as fast as she can.
You, who know me, know how trivial and
commonplace these domestic affections and
afflictions seem to me. It is not so with John
Lyne; he is absorbed in anxiety and grief.
Moreover he has suffered much in health; he
has become what I used most to hate—'an ill
man;' but I do not hate him yet. One does not
hate, ever, the man that has first brought the
light into one's life. . . . And with his illness,
his anxiety, his grief, he somehow has increased
his demands; he is not content to be my play-
fellow. The situation is serious: what am I
to do? Now that I write it in this brutal
way it has an ugly look. I must elucidate.

Elsie, attend to this! One afternoon last
week I met 'the bailiff,' not by accident, and,
I suppose, gave him—let us figure it thus—a
presumptive right to be jealous. When we
parted I added—shall we call it an order?—
to come up to Whiteknyghts in the evening.
There intervened an unfortunate moment, for
which the temerity of my town admirer is
responsible. Here's the account.

Returning home, I met Mr. Denham, leading his horse! John's eyes had been quicker than mine; he had spied him coming from the Court, where he had been to inquire for my uncle, who chanced to be better that afternoon. He had said to me, 'There is Mr. Denham!' I had answered, as we stood together there beneath our ash-tree, that it was impossible: 'He is in London still,' I had told him, and I believed I spoke the truth. Mr. Denham, riding from the Court, had tried a short cut which the snow disguised; his horse had stumbled over some pitfall of the waste land, and was badly lamed. Recall that I was happy and at peace with all the world; recall that Mr. Denham was glad of the accident which had so far hindered his return as to let him have a chance of seeing me. Understand that we were not far from the Whiteknyghts stable and a very long distance from Denham. You will conclude that, almost of necessity, I asked him back to the Court. For you would have done so yourself, light-hearted.

He was unaffectedly concerned, at first, about his horse; I had no danger signals. We walked along side by side, and I was thinking of 'the bailiff.' I forget, Elsie, when I first perceived that Mr. Denham was talking at all! I do remember that he said I did not look cold. And I laughed because, for some unknown reason, I was feeling at that instant much like a live torch. There is a warmth which has not to do with weather.

He went with his horse to the stable; I betook myself to his lordship's room, and interested him as far as I could in the Hon. Launce's misadventure. Ill-chanced that access of zeal :—'I should like to see him,' said my uncle.

He had been denied admission before, because it is a rule of the house : indeed he had only left his card ; but now that he was with us, my aunt descended to see him. She was enraptured with her own appearance, and consequently cordial—his visit happened to cheer the invalid. In fine, his horse being installed, the trap that was to have taken him back to

Denham was counter-ordered, and he remained to dinner.

Hardly, Elsie, can you conceive the change it made in our dull routine, this impromptu invitation. Lord Grenvers was wheeled into the dining-room, and her ladyship and I made those fancy-dress toilettes one makes in England when one says, 'We will not dress this evening.' Mr. Denham put on an elaborate array of my uncle's while his wet clothes were dried. And whether it was from the novelty of the costume or from the rarity of the circumstances, he became interesting. Of course we had many London topics in common, he and I : no doubt it was because of that. But I have left off trying to find out a reason for anything. Facts—facts only !

We dine at a punctual eight, and the meal is not a long one. At a quarter past nine his lordship was taken back to his own rooms, suffering slight premonitory symptoms of neuralgic pain. My aunt, in her familiar *rôle* of the 'Angel in the House,' floated out by the side of his chair, and waved a momentary '*à tantôt.*'

'I will be back directly,' she said; 'if you will have no more wine, Waldine will take you to her *sanctum:* let us have our coffee there together.'

Elsie, when she had left the room, I felt a wave of fear pass over me. In the warmth, the waxlight, the fragrance of fruit and flowers, the sense of *bien-être* in the charming room, the complete immunity from interruption, was there not every incentive to help this young man, never over-reticent, to speak his mind?

He fortified himself with another glass of claret: not to be formal, I got up and stood by the fire. 'Ah!' he said, 'it was almost too good to be true that I should see you sitting opposite to me like that at dinner.'

'It was not the first time,' I replied, but I felt the evasion was a poor one; it gave him too good a chance of saying that he hoped it would not be the last—the sort of repartee to which he is equal, and of which he availed himself with *empressement*.

I know! you can stop your ears and shut your eyes; blind and deaf you could give our brilliant dialogue almost word for word. He was very anxious to be serious, I was quite determined to be trivial. But when he asked point-blank to be let speak to me, half to gain time and half from inadvertence I told him I would permit his cigarette in my own sitting-room : I hoped that my aunt, having consigned her dear saint to his nurses and powdered her lovely nose, might be there before us, in order to arrange the lights for her complexion. She was not there : she had sent a hand-maiden to shroud the lamps becomingly : the room looked curiously warm and almost oriental. I never have the curtains drawn there, *pour des raisons;* and the pink and white candle shades told well against the black background of window glass. Perhaps the sight was cosy and pretty to envious eyes without. But how should Mr. Denham think of any such contingency? Nor did I, at the moment; I was intent on evading a definite demand. And this demand I *have* hitherto evaded.

It was twenty-five minutes past nine : think

that any one who waited outside my window since nine o'clock, had waited in the snow for nearly half an hour! And then think of this :—

Mr. Denham had dined well : Mr. Denham wanted to ask me to be his wife. I had brought him to a place where there was even less fear of interruption than in the dining-room, and, as there, we were alone. Add that Mr. Denham is not diplomatic, he is engagingly sincere, and you will not be unprepared for what occurred. He followed me closely into the room : we had exhausted conversation, and although we were not even looking at each other, to an observer our intimacy must have seemed assured. I stooped to fasten the case of my violin, which was lying on the floor, for fear my aunt's long train should catch the lid, when she came down. Mr. Denham seized the opportunity to see what sort of figure he made in a large looking-glass, which is over the fireplace. When I glanced up at the same glass, as I rose, I was greatly amused by his evident pleasure at the way my uncle's lounging-suit became him. I burst out laughing; I had quite forgotten I was close to my admirer in the flesh; I was only taken up by his image in the glass. Did he read delight in my mirth? In a moment he had caught me in his arms and I felt the breath of his lips upon my hair. . . .

No, he did not kiss me. I would have resisted that to the death. But the worst of it was that my escape from his salute was not due to any act of intrepidity on my part, but simply to the noiseless entrance at this juncture of Aunt Ethelinda. I did not even have to move aside, my gallant swain caught the scent of her approach and loosed me.

Elsie, from outside this is what it seemed: a sudden embrace interrupted by an unwelcome relative. And I knew for certain I could not appeal to my aunt. I saw, from her completely ignoring the proximity in which she found us, that her one regret was that she had not delayed her coming five minutes longer. Even as it was she was delighted. As for Launcelot, what had he to be ashamed of? he wished to astonish me, to take my bashful sense by storm. He would have tried it again had the opportunity occurred. I was not ashamed myself: he is not trifling with me: he has said quite enough to teach me that I may accept him at any moment and in any manner: nor had I behaved ill: I had been just civil to a man who does not displease me. That was all. But for the burning heart outside, in weariness and cold, was there no shame in this? Elsie, there was a man before my window whose soul was ashamed of me.

I did not see him; I had no chance of explanation.

I know that he was there: had I not bade him come? He turned and went away.

Do you care for the sequel of that evening? Lord Grenvers was worse, and Aunt Linda had come to make a courteous *adieu* to our unexpected guest. In a quarter of an hour he had left us, and she, really anxious for once, had returned to my uncle.

What did I do? I opened the window and stepped out upon the terrace in the snow. Oh!

once, for one last time, let me strip bare to you
my heart of hearts, and tell you what I did. So
soon the falling fleece would mar those careful
footsteps! I traced them while I could; I
followed towards the park. I came to a small
flight of steps where one goes down from the
gardens; you can see a mile before you there;
I strained my eyes, but he was out of sight.
I stooped and kissed the hand-rail where his
hand had rested, but it was cold already.
The stone of it said, '*No*,' through my lips to
my life. . . .

It is an old story now! I will not be
moved by it again: I pitied myself for a
while. Now I know that it was all for the
best; at least I hear you say so. But then I
pitied myself. I think that I was mad with
passion and shame. I had wanted so, that
night of all others, to tell him how I loved
him! I felt one throb of fever. I drank the
snow from his footprints!—But it is days
and days ago, and all is over.

I ought to have pitied *him*. He went
back to his lonely home and his dying mother

in the murk blackness of the night. Did he feel the irrevocable as I did, or did he trust me better than I trust myself? That icy wind! it seemed to lay Death's fingers on my love. I have not seen him since. I have suffered, I half forget how.

Elsie, I have written too much. I am not well, and we are an anxious household. It is as if a shadow brooded over us these winter days. Under the wings of that shadow what boon is brought me? Is it life? Is it love? I think it cannot be both.

I pull myself together to end my letter; the pen has outrun me. I meant to patch you up my life and live under that same patchwork. And so I will. I have not told you all, but I have told you something that will help you to understand me, whichever way I act. My resolve is, believe me, to do what is right. I began to write falsely; let me say truly, at least, now, that I am

Your true friend,

WALDINE DE STAIR.

February 8th.—I have just heard that John

Lyne's mother died this evening. I have not heard it from himself; but I think he will tell me his wish; they say that he is going away. But news comes shrouded here. Elsie, my uncle cannot live till spring. The story of my sojourn here is almost done.

CHAPTER VII.

A FAREWELL

THIS was John's letter at last :—

February 12th.

WALDINE, my Love—

I buried my mother to-day; if I seem to have told you nothing you will the easier forgive me by and by. Say, at least, 'He kept his troubles from me.' Say that when I am gone.

If I can do so, let me tell you facts; it is what you bade me do.

The worst fact first : I saw you in the arms of a man who—I suppose—would laugh if I should call myself his rival. It is now many days ago, but I see you still. I shall see you so until I die.

Second fact, harder to write. I do not blame

you : I do not misunderstand. I have thought it out. You knew that I was there : you would have spared me this. You were not—are not —bad enough to dismiss me by these means.

But dismiss me you did. Third fact, which hangs from these: I am going to leave England at once. My only love, it is the only way. I sail by the ship *Valentine* on St. Valentine's Day—'tis an omen. . . . I can't put words together : you freeze the lava of speech, and in my heart there is no heat against you. It is right for you to marry Denham. There, that is said. It was the hardest thrust of all, that sword thrust of conviction.

Look how I trust your word ! I do not leave you choice : I go before you can stay me. I know that you would come, but to your life-long sorrow. You love me, do you not ? Ah yes ! you love me, but I love you better than you ever loved me. I will die without you sooner than let you live for me. How should it not come home to you at last what might have been? When I am gone, forget me. You will suffer a little, but you will know (so

soon!) that I was right. If I could doubt that
Denham loved you! . . . But now I cannot.

And I am a dying man. If you did come
with me, it would only be for a few months, and
it would unmake all your life. Oh! if I live or
die, forget me; remember only that I loved you
well. So well, Waldine—so well—so well!

The words break my spirit. . . . You will
forget or will remember as you choose.

If you will do something for me, take care
of my parents' grave. I would to God—that
after death—the death I go to meet abroad
alone—I too might lie there. If you would
do me some great thing, contrive me this.

My queen, my child, I am gone! to-
morrow night I sail. Almost I am glad to be
ridding you of such a burthen. Don't be
sorry: I do not need to say this is not want
of love. It is the one thing that a man who
loves you best can do that is best for you.

For me? . . . Darling, there is a star in
my soul always: I kissed you first.

JOHN LYNE.

CHAPTER VIII.

THE FLASHED RECALL

AND this Waldine's reply :—

'To JOHN LYNE, S.S. *Valentine*,
    Plymouth.

  To-morrow | night | at | nine | the | Willow | Garth.'

No other word, she knew it was enough. The telegram was sent from a post-office, some miles distant, to which she had gone for information on the routes abroad which could not be obtained at Netherfield. And there was no reply: it was a command, not a prayer, from a hand which held the issues of life and death.

He could not reach Netherfield direct by the cross journey, but he came to the terminus at Newton, within five leagues, and walked through the declining day.

CHAPTER IX.

[AND LAST]

FULFILMENT

A MAN and woman face to face alone. St. Valentine's Eve.

Night in the Willow-Garth: winter night as soft as spring: over the old familiar meeting-place the old familiar moon, no doubt, but shrouded from their eyes.

Underfoot the bedded leaves: about and around the waste of waters filled with melted February snows. All dark, all still, all wrapped in gloom like the grave's.

So often they had met here of late. Further from John's home than from hers—out of all human ken—its solitude seldom broken, the strange place had lent them a trysting spot from the very first. Waldine could have felt her way through the tangle blindfold. Beneath the larches that enclosed the garth there was a little stem of blood-red maple which had kept its leaves all through the frosty weather : it had been her beacon a thousand times, had saved her from the perils of that marshy tract where a false step had landed her so nearly.

And there was shelter for the lovers in the thick-set, wind-proof copse. There was the old boathouse with the half-sunk punt in it which would never carry Lord Grenvers any more, in his favourite wild fowl shooting, but which was for ever sacred from profane hands as a record of his liking and his skill. It stood on the very marge of the lake, and the waters round it were reedy and deep. The wooden shed was fallen in disrepair : the door swung loose upon its hinges : one fold of it had dropped already, and lay stretched across the wrecked boat.

Against the lintel of that door John Lyne was standing. He leaned there overpowered with fatigue—with hunger too, poor normal need of life ! he had not tasted food that day.

An immense joy was upon him : to reach the presence of his idol, that was his heart's desire. But there had supervened on this a numbness that was new.

He had waited for her a weary hour : now at last she was here. His famished sight could feast upon her beauty, his thirsty lips on her fair face. Such a contrast as they made ! John, travel-worn and tired—a big, gaunt figure in his mourning clothes ; Waldine with rich furs draping her to her feet, yet not wholly hiding her white evening dress. Her cheeks were pale under the feathered shade of her velvet hat, and by nearness to the black lace twisted round her neck. But her eyes were like bright lights in the gloom : they were full of pride and power : one could feel that they only veiled laughter, whereas for John's set mouth the laughing days were done. He held her in his arms once more : he felt the seal-skin of her coat soft and warm against his stiff hands, he felt her breath upon his chin, her fingers on his neck. In his ears was the music of her voice, so many days desired.

'What did you think of me?' she said, speaking quickly and low—'husband, ever dearest love, had you not my word that I was yours? Oh! to tell you all! it has seemed to me, these empty hours, as if the web of life were closing round me, as if I soon should be only a poor woven image of a woman in the loom of the world. Now I have cut the threads: I am alive once more! You want me, do you not?—you did not wish to escape me. . . . How I must love you, how I must know you love me, never to dream of that! My strength, my master, I will go with you to the end of the world.'

'I wanted you,' said John, 'as one wants heaven. I did all I could for the world's poor best. But God is too good for us: the world's poor best is vile.'

'Do not despise the world,' she said and laughed; 'we will make something of it between us. I am so sanguine, John. I have no fears. See! we must learn reason: there are plans to be made. Tell me all you have done from the very beginning.'

'I am gone,' said John, smiling in spite of the deathly fatigue and illness that was upon him,—so magnetic was her will :—'the only strangeness is that I am here. I have taken my farewell of Netherfield: it seemed not hard, with all that I have lost. And I had paved the way ere now, in case we went together by and by : Waldine, you are not afraid ? You will come with me ? It is for life or death.'

'Need you ask it ? But to-night the ship must sail away without you. Never mind your things ! Let them drift to America, we shall find them there. Why have you taken me at unawares ? I have no scheme of action ready. Is poor Aunt Linda's providence to work it all ? Dispose of me as you will, my hero !'

Only a heavy sigh for answer.

'John, you have no courage ! you are cold.' —She freed herself and looked him in the face.—'What is it ? are you tired—or are you ill ?' There was a note of impatience in her tone which did not escape him ; he knew all her changes.

'Aye, that's it,' he said softly at last with

a great sigh. 'It's the old grievance, beloved, which you never cared to hear. But it is only to-night I am so tired. The heaviness will pass, the joy abide. Plans, Waldine? yes, but let me look at you first. My wife, how beautiful you are! how strong, how dainty! Ah! the regrets I ought to feel for that poor London that is robbed of you for ever now; but I have none. . . . From the first, Waldine, from the very first! There is no face in all the world but this face of yours for me. Oh! for life together!—but not here—not here!' . . .

'Dear, I have been thoughtless of you! not for the first time. How often I must have come here these last weeks to meet you, pampered and warm, while you have been cold and starved, in failing health! John, I have never thought of this at all till now. I will make amends—amends? Have I not power enough for both. Ah! this is not fatigue; it is a faintness that is on you—the journey, the long day, the griefs that you have suffered. And now the waiting and the happiness. . . . I have been blind and selfish always!

Let me begin anew. . . . Answer me! John!
Oh! God in heaven. . . . Here!—your head
upon my heart. Love, answer! Speak!'—

He had slowly sunk upon his knees, his
hands still clasped about her. She tore open
her jacket and pressed his head upon her
bosom with a desperate instinct, new born in
her mind, to give him back the warmth of which
her will had robbed him. Her brain was fire;
the wild thoughts surged in it—unformed,
beyond control. She had no definite hope,
but just to save him and renew his strength.
With her lips to his eyes, her arms round his
body, she held him up in an embrace that was
like life. It could not leave him senseless.

'Mine—mine'—he said at last: and
then——

They were on the brink of the lake; he
had slipped a little on the reed-grown bank,
and she, now kneeling forwards to dip her
hand in the icy stream for his refreshment,
felt that it was only by her force that she
prevented his fall. One foot was caught
already in the sedge, and one hand, loosing

her, sought vaguely, weakly, for the boathouse door. It was quite dark; the sky
black, whence some star of help should be
born. There was not the light of a wild-
flower on those banks that would grow forget-
me-not in spring.

'To-morrow'—he said, as the gloom closed
over his eyes, and tried to lift his lips to hers
for one last kiss that should slake more than
thirst.

And even with that word he had fallen
from the girl's grasp into deep water.

It seemed to her, for one sharp instant, as
of Death's, that her very soul had left her.
She gave a sort of moan that was never made
a cry; and passionately, madly snatched his
left arm as the stream engulfed him. But
the faintness that had seized him left his
limbs quite irresponsive to her grasp. . . .

And then—what was it? fate? chance?
will? She let go his arm and buried her face
in her hands. She would not save him, but
she could not see him die.

The solution of Death! It was the only

way. Her entire being would have revolted
from it as a scheme, but as a fact she accepted
it without a sigh. What was there she could
do? She was not unconscious; her strong
nerves never failed her; the water was not
hell enough to drown her had she made one
vigorous effort. She did not make it; she
obeyed her lot, success. It was to be!

'Best so,' she said at last—it was long after—
and stayed upon dry land.

Not otherwise she could have killed him: she
was made of flame, not mud: she was no common
murderess. But thus, by this calm death, she
let him perish. Was there any lot on earth
that could have soothed him half so well?

The grim weeds held him fast, the place
was just his grave, no more. As at last, ashen
white, she rose to her feet, her hand stirred
the old punt a little, which his fall had pushed
aside; it settled back into its place again,
undisturbed for many years, over his loving
heart. Thus time withholds eternity.

There was no trace of him left: with him
had sunk the few poor things he had—his

watch, his money, his cigar-case; had anything been left it might have moved her to
some human outcry, to some vain trial of her
strength, some disclosure which must have
shamed her for ever. But there was nothing.
What he left her was an immaterial cross.
To take up her racked martyr-life for the sake
of the world's thorn crown. It sounds—or
should sound—hard; but was it? Who shall
answer? Perhaps it was the easiest way, as
well as best: the key to such a riddle is not
here. God holds it.

When she stood up she did not feel
remorse: her one sensation was of a great
difficulty evaded, an infinite freedom won.
The heart-break would come later; her instinct now was to escape the past. To stay
here, to behold this place again, that were
madness,—at least that way madness lay.

She did not tarry: the whole tragedy had
taken less than an hour. It was a clean
knife-cut across the thread of the winter's life.
The man that had taught her love lay dead in
the woodland like a wild thing shot or a

frozen bird. As for her. . . . She had knelt on her dark furs; there was no stain upon her dress !

A spring of life seemed bounding in her breast; she shook herself clear of the low undergrowth, stooped through the willows and ran out of the wood. Something white and ghostly stared at her forth of the dark. It was the dog's grave.

On the white wood of which she knew the words, 'Death looseth.'

Before she had been many minutes in her room, a light footfall sounded in the passage and Lady Grenvers entered, in studied disarray. 'Dear Val,' she said, 'I do neglect you so: I have not been near you this evening. And I can't go to bed without telling you something most important. Launcelot Denham has written to my poor saint about you.—"To be your Valentine."—It is such an enchantment to us both. You will not refuse him. The prospect of the wedding is *fresh life* to me, though I ought to be thinking of—but who thinks of death for long, ever? . . . Horrid!— I promised not to tell you, but I must. You would know anyway—alas! so soon— Val, you know I never cared for the country —and Launce, though he is rich, has no house. Grenvers is leaving you White-knyghts by will; on condition that—after your marriage—you make this place your home. Sleep upon that! How fresh and cool your cheek is!—Dear—Good-night!'

THE END.

G., C., & Co.

Printed by R. & R. CLARK, *Edinburgh.*

www.ingramcontent.com/pod-product-compliance
Lightning Source LLC
Chambersburg PA
CBHW020115030726
47498CB00006B/2117